Copyright © 2025 E S Monk

Published 2025

ISBN 9798291011560

Brambleberry Wedding

By

E.S. Monk

Isobel

Isobel traced the intricate gold letters on the ivory-coloured linen invitation with her finger.

Charles Finlay & Eleanor Riggs

Request the pleasure of your company

To celebrate their marriage

She looked up, turning to the window and taking in the sprawling view of New York City that her high-rise apartment offered her. On that cold, overcast February day, her heart slumped in her chest.

It was all she'd ever dreamed of. The high-flying career in finance – check. Being headhunted by one of the top companies in New York – check. The most spectacular apartment in one of the most prestigious areas of the city, courtesy of her employment package – check. The vast pay check hitting her bank account every month – check. Buying her first house last year, an exquisite country cottage in the Cotswolds back home in England – check. The relentless hours, pushing herself and excelling in every way she possibly could in order to pursue her goals and manoeuvre her career towards the next step, always driven and always wanting more... *'When will it ever be enough?'* she whispered aloud to herself.

It was almost two months ago, in December, when the world she had so carefully, almost forensically constructed, slowly began to unravel. It started when she reconnected with her father, Charlie. Her relationship with him had always been somewhat strained. Truth be told, she barely knew him as a child. He was what her mother called 'a workaholic.' He provided substantially for her and her mother. She'd attended the best schools in the area, her clothes and accessories where always the envy of her friends, and she was one hundred percent indulged with her only passion outside of academic work - horses. As a youngster, she'd lived for her twice weekly riding lessons, Saturday pony club, and holiday clubs at the local riding stables. So it wasn't that he didn't love her - she always knew deep down that he did. He was just never there. But she got used to it because that's just how things where. And she had her mother, who doted on her only daughter, and even to this day, Isobel would count her as one of her closest friends and confidantes. After her parents divorced when she was fourteen, she saw less and less of her father, until he seemed to have just phased slowly but surely out of her life. She'd excelled at school and transitioned easily to Cambridge University where she studied mathematics and business. She devoured her university lectures hungrily, always keen for extra work, eager to be the best in her class, which she was. Her professors spoke highly of her and with some wonderful references under her belt, she stepped into the world of business, excelling everywhere she went. Isobel worked day and night, until one day, the phone call came just after she'd turned twenty-eight, offering her the position of Chief Financial Adviser for one of the most prestigious companies in New York.

Isobel thought back fondly as the memory of that very phone call sprung into her mind. *I had everything.*

For the next two and half years, Isobel continued her relentless work ethic, earning herself a formidable reputation as the company expanded, and with it, a generous rise in her pay check.

After her first twelve months in New York, Isobel ticked off one of the major goals she'd set herself on the day she'd graduated from university. She owned her own home. As soon as she'd been able to do so, she'd taken out a mortgage and got herself on the property ladder. She'd chosen a small, beautiful character cottage back in England, in the same village her mother and stepfather had chosen to settle in after their wedding ten years ago. The location enabled her mother to keep an eye on it so she could let it out as a holiday cottage. Her gradual increase of salary over the years, plus her substantial bonuses, and her frugal spending habits had enabled her to pay off the mortgage in full, by the time she turned twenty-nine. It was then that she felt her life was amounting to something, and that her years of hard work were paying off. She felt settled in New York, loved the company she worked for and thrived off the demands of her job, and now, being mortgage-free, she had plenty of money available to enable her to tick another item off her list of goals. This item always seemed like an indulgence, but even at the age of twenty-one, just after completing her degree when her list was written and she was champing at the bit to plunge herself into the corporate world, she couldn't help but tag it on the end. Isobel wanted her very own horse. A childhood of wishing for her own pony but only ever been able to enjoy riding school ponies fuelled Isobel's desire to add her adolescent dream to her list.

Christopher was a bright bay, sixteen hand, warmblood gelding. He was kept on full livery, at a beautiful yard just outside the city. The half-mile driveway was flanked by immaculate post and rail fences, each horse enjoying twenty-four hours turn out in their individual paddocks. The stables were light and airy, the indoor sand school was perfect for all year-round training and jumping, and the yard boasted one hundred acres of unspoilt private land for hacking, plus plenty of options to ride further afield if needed. The amount her beloved horse cost her on a monthly basis could easily have afforded her a second property!

Isobel felt like her life was ticking along nicely. She spent every available hour working, apart from her two or three trips to the yard every week. Work/life balance – check.

Her father had reconnected with her about six months ago. Although his first email came completely out of the blue, and she had to admit, it took her a little while to come to terms with welcoming him back into her life, she was pleased to rebuild their relationship. The first five months had been spent emailing and letter writing, and their correspondence had been enjoyable, but by no means a distraction from her work, or Christopher. But then she'd invited him and his girlfriend Eleanor, to come over and spend Christmas with her, and that is when her seemingly perfect life suddenly became not so perfect. Far from it in fact.

Isobel knew her father hadn't done it deliberately. He'd just tried to explain, as best he could, the constant gnawing hunger he'd felt, driving him, relentlessly, to succeed. And how he'd sacrificed so much, including his marriage to her mother, and his relationship with her, is only child, in order to feed his career-driven hunger. He apologised, profusely, for his absence in her life. And he explained to her how he regretted the many years he'd missed out on being a father to her, and that in the end, he realised that his career just hadn't been worth it. Then he shared how he'd taken a sabbatical, rented a little cottage in Cornwall and met Eleanor.

Having now met Eleanor, Isobel could see why her father had fallen so easily for her. She wasn't like him, or Isobel for that matter, in any way, shape or form. Eleanor seemed to float through life easily, gently and seemingly able to deal with whatever life threw at her, and still thrive. She lived for the small things. Her beloved little donkey, Rupert. Her artwork, her little Cornish cottage and garden, and her walks across the moors to enjoy watching the wild ponies graze. There was absolutely nothing power-hungry about Eleanor. Isobel adored her as soon as she met her and was absolutely thrilled when her father and Eleanor got engaged.

It was once the excitement of seeing her father again, the wonderful Christmas holiday they shared, and the marvellous news of the engagement simmered down, that she felt it. She found her mind begin to wander at work, something that had never happened before. But little thoughts kept creeping into her mind about what it might be like to be in love so deeply that you would choose to spend the rest of your life with that person. Thoughts of what it might be like to come home to a husband after work, and maybe even a child...or two. Thoughts that if her fictional children came to life, then maybe she would only work part time. And it would be her that a husband came home too. A big, messy, child-filled house, with a dog or two romping around her spacious, child-friendly garden. And her children would have a pony, a friend for Christopher. She even caught herself staring at children playing in the park, and couples holding hands strolling around the city.

It was over the past seven weeks that the unsettling feeling, deep within her, had steadily grown from a little ding of a triangle to an all-out marching band. To begin with, she had tried to block it out. She kept herself busy and pushed herself even harder at work, but to no avail. And so, she tried a different tack. She welcomed the feelings, thinking that maybe it was just a phase and if she faced the unfamiliar emotions head on, she could deal with them and move forward. But all that did was intensify them, telling her, loudly and clearly, that she was no longer living her dream life, and a little voice in her head piped up. *You heard what your father said. You don't want to end up like him and feel you've missed out on life because all you did was work.*

Harry

Harry looked down at the photograph he was holding in his hand, and there, smiling back at him was Adele. He gently touched her sun-kissed cheek with his finger and sighed.

"Calling all passengers for flight 236 to Heathrow, London. We are now ready for you to board the plane," boomed a voice over the airport tanoy.

Carefully, he folded the photograph in half, then in half again. Slinging his backpack over his shoulder, he stood up, then hesitating for only a moment, tossed the photograph into the bin.

"Good afternoon, Sir, please may I see your boarding pass?" asked the smiling flight attendant.

He fumbled, rather awkwardly, to retrieve the pass with his left hand from his backpack; his right arm currently sporting a plaster cast from a rather unfortunate event six weeks ago.

Immediately after taking his designated seat, he plugged in his earphones, turned up the volume on his iPod, tilted his hat over his eyes, and drowned out the world around him. At that precise moment, it was just enough that he had to tolerate his own company, let alone a plane full of chattering passengers, and a rather nosy-looking lady seated to the left of him. Small talk on this long-haul flight was most definitely off the cards.

He'd been living in Australia for two months shy of two years, supposedly living his best life. Well that's what he'd kept telling everyone back home. But now, here he was, tail tucked firmly between his legs, scuttling back, with the hope that his brother would forgive him.

To be fair, he told himself, *the first twelve months were the most wonderful adventure.*

His beautiful Australian girlfriend, Adele, had taken him to her sprawling 300,000-acre family cattle ranch, two hundred kilometres east of Alice Springs, in the Northern Territory. After the initial shock that their beloved daughter had returned after her six months trip travelling around Europe with an English boyfriend in tow, her family had welcomed him keenly, especially when they found out that not only could he ride, but he could also train horses and work cattle.

It was after the honeymoon period that it had all started to go wrong. They'd had six months of working hard on the ranch, coupled with impromptu bouts of chucking a tent and backpack in the back of her pick-up and taking off for a week or so at a time to explore the bush, but then things began to unravel. And it also had to do with Adrian, Adele's boyfriend. Well, not exactly her boyfriend. They'd spilt up before she set off on her travels. She even admitted that he was the reason she booked her ticket and left Australia. She'd told him that things just hadn't worked out. But once Harry had become part of the furniture around the place, and got friendly with the other workers, they'd let slip on one particularly drunken evening that there had been a bit more to it than that. They'd been childhood sweethearts and, madly in love with Adele, Adrian had proposed. The story went that she panicked, told her parents she needed to get away, booked her ticket to Milan, Italy, with a couple of friends, and vanished for six months. A very confused, heartbroken Adrian was left in her wake.

And then he met Adrian at a social dance that the whole family had been invited too He wanted to feel smug. To know that he'd got the beautiful girl, and he was living his happy ever after - bad luck to Adrian. But he couldn't. He actually liked the man. He was a decent, down-to-earth Aussie, who in any other circumstances Harry would probably have become friends with. And then there was the way they looked at each other. He'd followed Adele's gaze across the busy dance floor, and he knew, deep down, that he didn't stand a chance. She'd never looked at him like that, and quite frankly, he felt like the gooseberry of the uncomfortable little trio he seemed to have unwittingly found himself within.

Harry and Adele had limped on for another eight months. *Pathetic,* he tutted to himself, as he thought about it. But he'd upped and left his life for her, dropping Tom, his brother and business partner, like a stone, and he didn't want to give up too easily...and he wasn't ready to go crawling back to his brother quite so soon.

For the last six months he'd travelled from ranch to ranch, taking on short term contracts training horses and droving cattle, all the while burying his head in the sand, refusing to allow himself to acknowledge all the responsibilities he'd so recklessly left far away, at home, in Cornwall.

When Christmas came around, he'd had no choice but to put on a fake smile and phone his brother to wish him a merry Christmas. He might have been rather cowardly with his reluctance to return, and even admit the truth to his brother, but he wasn't so awful that he couldn't pretend, just for a quick phone call, that Tom's sacrifice in letting him leave with his blessing had not been wasted. But on hearing his brother's familiar voice, and learning of the nightmare he was living through, his heart sank. Tom's house was currently a building site and uninhabitable, in the middle of winter, due to a delayed phone call to the plumber because of his overflowing workload. All Harry could do in response to the news was to blunder through what a great time he was having before swiftly hanging up the phone, and promptly turning into a blubbering mess over his current poor life choices.

And the poor life choices kept coming. The finest of those choices being the decision to get roaringly drunk on New Years Eve with a gang of fellow ranch hands. The evening culminated in a competition to see who could take two shots of whiskey, climb the ladder onto a tin roof of questionable stability on a rickety shed outside the pub, whilst carrying a pint, down the pint at the top, and then repeat. And that is how he found himself in hospital, with the hangover of all hangovers. The doctors told him how stupid he had been, how he could have killed himself, and that he was very lucky indeed. Apparently, he'd knocked himself out with the fall, but other than the broken arm and superficial cuts and bruises, there was no major harm done.

Lying in that hospital bed for three days gave him plenty of time to think. And he continued to think as he slowly hitch-hiked, in a rather zig-zag fashion, across Australia, until he ended up right outside Sydney airport on the fifth of February.

A wave of nausea washed over Harry as he thought about what he'd done Tom. Their mother had been unwell, and after moving to Spain for her health, his parents had left Hill Valley Stables in the capable hands of their two sons, who had both keenly assured them that they one hundred percent wanted to take over the family riding school and horse training business, together, as a partnership. Yet at the first sight of a gorgeous Aussie girl, Harry had only given Tom twenty-four hours' notice that he was emigrating to the other side of the world. And to make his guilty conscience even worse, his big brother had shaken his hand, slapped him on the back and wished him all the best.

Thoughts of the past filled his mind throughout the whole flight, as he slipped in and out of fitful sleep. And now, having disembarked from the plane and trudged wearily through the airport, the queue at passport control was moving at a snail's pace. Harry shuffled along, earphones still firmly in place, avoiding eye contact at all costs. He then stood back as his fellow passengers scrambled amongst themselves to grab their bags off the carousel, and he proceeded to watch his own bag circulate, once, twice, three times, before he finally stepped forward to claim it. He could delay the inevitable no longer. Weaving his way between the throngs of people, he navigated the tail end of the airport, before finally stepping outside into the very traditional British wintery weather of murky grey clouds and rain. Not the type of plump, luscious raindrops that every other country seems to experience when it rains, but the wet, drizzly mess that permeates every inch of you, dampening your skin, your attire and your spirit. It was proper English rain.

He looked up at the sky, felt the icy drizzle prickling his skin, inhaled deeply, then marched purposefully towards the coach station. It was time to face the repercussions of his actions. It was time to go home.

Isobel

"What do you mean you're closed for a month!" cried Isobel over the phone. "Christopher is on his way to you now!"

Isobel paced up and down her mother's kitchen as she listened to the voice at the other end of the phone explaining that a horse on their yard had just been diagnosed with the seriously contagious horse virus, strangles. The yard was to be on lockdown for four weeks until the horse in question had recovered and deemed fit and healthy again. It was out of the question for any horse, even one who was currently in transit from America, to set foot on their yard whilst they were in quarantine.

Just as Isobel felt like she was going to have a mini nervous breakdown, the owner of the now closed yard offered her a sliver of hope.

"I've spoken to a friend of mine. He owns Hill Valley stables, it's about half an hour away from here, and he's happy for you to board Christopher at his yard whilst we wait the month out, or the full three months, whichever you prefer. I've informed the transport company, and they've agreed to take your horse directly to his yard. I can assure you that Christopher will be well looked after whilst he's there. I'm so terribly sorry for the inconvenience."

Isobel thanked the yard owner and put down the phone, then felt the familiar, comforting touch of her mother, as she folded her into her arms and squeezed her tightly.

"Everything will work itself out in the end," her mother whispered, before kissing the top of her head, then swiftly pulled away from their embrace. "Now, chop, chop," she said, ushering Isobel out of the kitchen. "There's lots to do before you leave for Cornwall."

Isobel, trying to gain control of the panic currently shooting through her veins at the speed of a rocket, clomped up the stairs to her mother's spare room, and began to pack.

She had been in a permanent state of anxiety ever since she'd walked into her boss's office fourteen days ago, and through embarrassingly messy sobs, explained her new outlook on life, before quitting her job on the spot. She then marched down to the local travel agents and booked both herself and Christopher one-way tickets to England. And then she'd called her mum.

Isobel was always a woman with a plan, but the plan was just going slightly awry at this very moment of time. As she focused on neatly folding the clothes she'd need for her stay in Cornwall, she tried to calm herself down by going through her projected course of action.

"One – get me and Christopher to Cornwall. Two – find out where Hill Valley stables is without a panic attack. Three – Explain to Dad that I'll be staying in Cornwall for the three months up until the wedding. Four – find somewhere to live over the next three months near Christopher. Five – make a plan for what happens after the wedding. Six - find a job to walk into when my extended holiday in Cornwall comes to an end. Seven - live happily ever after."

Isobel repeated her seven-step plan, over and over again, until her bags were packed, her heartbeat steadied, and her mum's spare room was spick and span.

Two hours later, Isobel was sipping a much-needed cup of tea and tucking into a Danish pastry at Exeter services when her phone rang. The company transporting Christopher called to update her on his journey, and to let her know that he would be arriving at his new destination, Hill Valley Stables, in approximately an hour and a half. Isobel checked the sat nav on her phone, if she left now, she should arrive at the same time. Glugging down her tea, she headed back out to the car her mother had loaned her and finally felt a smidgen of excitement about the new life unfolding ahead of her. No matter what happened, she and Christopher were in this together, and even though he was a horse, and not a person, just knowing that someone else was paddling alongside her, in their currently directionless boat, gave her comfort for their forthcoming journey.

Isobel's heart skipped a beat when she spotted the sign, Hill Valley stables, finally, after driving down the seemingly never-ending Cornish country lanes. As she directed her car through the gateway, she saw a smart horse lorry with its company's name sprawled across its flanks, parked in the yard. *He's here!*

As soon as she stepped out of her car, she was greeted with the excited yippity yip of a little Scottie dog, and bending down to say hello, an adorable yellow Labrador puppy tumbled into her, keen as mustard to be part of the welcoming committee.

"Mallie, Jewel, give her some space you daft dogs!"

Looking up, Isobel met the eyes of a friendly-looking woman.

"I'm Poppy," said the woman, bending down to scoop up the puppy. "And this is Jewel, my boyfriend Tom's puppy. And he's my little rascal," she continued, pointing to the Scottie dog. "His name's Mallie."

"How lovely to meet you all," replied Isobel, instantly feeling at ease after Poppy's warm welcome. "I'm Isobel." She gestured over to the lorry. "And my horse, Christopher, is in there."

"Let's get him out then!" said Poppy.

Heading over to the lorry, Poppy chatted ten to the dozen about how sad it was to hear about the nearby yard going down with strangles, how excited they all were to meet Christopher, and how terribly sorry she was that Tom wasn't there to meet her. He and his brother were out at the other end of the farm fixing some fencing, but she'd called him as soon as the lorry arrived so he should be back any minute.

"Wait," said Poppy, stopping so abruptly that Isobel almost walked right into her. "Isobel and Christopher?"

"Yes, that's right," Isobel replied cautiously.

"As in Charlie's Isobel and Christopher?"

How on earth would she know that? "Um, yes, I'm Charlie's daughter."

And then Isobel felt the full force of Poppy's arms wrapping her into a tight hug.

"Oh my gosh, this is so exciting, I can't believe I didn't put two and two together. Charlie and Eleanor have told me so much about you!"

Isobel felt like the only child at the party left without a seat during that dreadful game, musical chairs.

Picking up on Isobel's confusion, Poppy explained that

Brambleberry Cottage, where Eleanor and Charlie lived, was in the village just a couple of miles away. Eleanor was one of her closest friends, and it was Poppy who'd looked after Rupert, Eleanor's miniature donkey, whilst they visited Isobel in New York over Christmas.

Isobel had been in what she could only describe as a dream like state over the past couple of months, and her total self-absorption had left her with little ability or inclination to fully process the 'gossip' of her dad's and Eleanor's day to day life from their phone calls. As colour flushed her cheeks, the reluctant feeling of guilt swished through her. *I'm a selfish, horrible daughter...*

Both women's attention was diverted when they heard a man's voice cut through the air.

"Hello, sorry I'm late." Isobel looked up to see a man hurrying across the field ahead of them, saving her the embarrassment of explaining that now she had finally crawled out of her self-indulgent pity party, the names Poppy, Mallie and Tom, did in fact, ring a bell.

After introductions had been made, Tom finally got to the business of why she was actually there. As he lowered down the tailboard, she heard Christopher's familiar nicker from within, and then, there he was. Her beautiful horse, little ears pricked, eyes shining bright, as he took in his new environment. Right now, Isobel felt like he was her only true friend in the world. She climbed in, inhaled his comfortingly sweet horsey smell, clipped his lead rope on, and like a proud parent, led him on to the yard.

"Oh, wow," gushed Poppy.

"What a horse!" exclaimed Tom.

An hour later, Christopher was settled in his stable, and Isobel's designated area of the feed room was stacked to the brim with all his things. Somewhat reluctantly, she said her goodbyes to Poppy and Tom. It was time to go and explain herself to her father. She'd hoped to ease herself gently into learning to deal with her new way of life, and to go through the process privately. But that had been blown wide open now that her horse was being stabled at her father's friend's yard. The village grapevine would be in full swing, and no doubt Eleanor and her dad would know all about Christopher before she even arrived! He would have questions why she'd asked to pop in for a quick visit, when in fact, she'd walked away from her perfect life in New York, dragged her horse all the way from America and plonked him in a yard just walking distance from his home. It was time to step out of her bubble and face the music of her own creation.

Harry

Harry bashed the nail into the fencing steak with a strong thwack from his hammer. The monotonous work, at least, gave an outlet for his growing frustration. A frustration, he admitted to himself, watching his brother walk away across the field and back down to the yard to deal with the arrival of a new horse, which was completely unfounded.

Harry had been welcomed home by Tom like the prodigal son. He'd shaken his hand, slapped him on his back, and cracked open a couple of beers to celebrate his return. Harry felt nauseous just thinking about it. He didn't deserve any of it. Deep down he'd hoped his brother would have given him a good thump, square across the jaw, then it would have been over and done with. But he didn't. And now Harry was living in his self-imposed prison of guilt, and the kinder Tom was towards him, the further he burrowed into it.

There had been no talk of blaming Harry for the mess he'd left him in. No talk of how Harry could make it up to Tom, no threat of shunning Harry from the business. The morning after he'd arrived, it was business as usual from Tom. The regular discussions about which horses need to be exercised, which horses needed to be brought in for the farrier and a polite request to pick up the monthly feed bags from the local agricultural store. As if nothing had happened. As if Harry had never left.

Whack. Another nail bashed in. He stood up to stretch his aching back, and gazed across the lush fields of green, a far cry from the sun-baked outback land he'd become accustomed to, and he knew that he was home. That was one thing Harry did know; he never intended to leave Hill Valley stables again.

In the stillness of the countryside air, he heard a gate click, diverting his attention from the patchwork quilt of fields spanning the horizon. Riding towards him was Tom, on his jet-black thoroughbred, Billy, leading Walter, one of the riding school horses.

"Want to go riding?" Tom called out.

The brothers fell into step, side by side on their horses, as they ambled along the country lanes, the rhythmical beat of the horse's iron clad shoes on the tarmac beneath them filling the silence.

"You really screwed me over," announced Tom.

Finally! thought Harry.

"Poppy suggested I don't say anything. That life is too short, and we should just put it all behind us and move on. But she's a much nicer human being than me!" he said with a wry laugh.

Harry privately agreed. What he'd learned about Poppy in the short time he'd spent with her, was that his brother was a very lucky man indeed to have found such a lovely, down-to-earth girlfriend. She was far nicer than what's her name who'd cleared off and left him for pastures new all those years ago. And then a thought hit him, smack bang in the gut. The ex had left him. Their parents upped and left to move to Spain, and then Harry had buggered off and left him. And it was Tom who'd been left alone, Tom who'd quietly and steadfastly got on with his work and continued to run their so-called family business.

"I'm sorry, Tom," replied Harry sincerely. "Want to punch me?"

"Yes!" said his brother, "but Poppy would be furious with me. And you aren't worth getting into trouble with her for!"

Harry guided Walter behind Tom when he directed Billy off the lane and onto the single file track that would lead them to the woods. Harry knew what was coming. They'd ridden this path hundreds of times, and right on cue, Tom picked up the pace. In no time at all, the brothers were hurtling along the woodland tacks, weaving between the trees, jumping anything in their path.

The horses snorted and danced as they were slowed to navigate the narrow brook and gateway that left the density of trees behind them, and miles of sparse, open moorland ahead. *Nothing beats the unspoilt countryside of Cornwall.*

"Race you!" shouted Tom, and then he was gone.

Harry's reliable riding school horse was no match for Billy, and Tom knew it! All Harry could do was watch the speed machine that was Billy accelerate into the distance. Tom slowed, allowing Harry to catch up, and they cantered steadily alongside one another, just like they used to do when they were children.

The horses cooled down as they meandered along the quiet lanes back towards the stables, and as Walter's breathing steadied, Harry felt a calmness spread through the horse, then slowly seep within himself. The air between him and Tom had been cleared, and now it was time to move forward, and with that in mind, he finally felt ready to broach the subject with his brother.

"I noticed there's a horse sale on Saturday, I thought I might take a look," he said tentatively, trying to gauge his brother's response. But Tom gave nothing away. And so, he continued. "I have some savings," he started, just make sure his brother knew he wasn't looking for a handout. "I could get a couple of youngsters to train and sell on?"

"Fill your boots. The business always needs an injection of cash!" laughed Tom. "How quickly would the turn around be?"

This is what Harry had missed. This is what Harry unknowingly ached for during his lost years in Australia. Talking business with his brother. Family business.

"We should have money in the bank in a couple of months."

The sun was all but set when they turned into their driveway. Harry could see the lights on in the house. A pang of loneliness swept through him. He knew that Poppy wasn't working in the village pub this evening, so she'd be busy cooking Tom's supper. He'd have to find somewhere else to live. Now that Tom had Poppy, he knew it wouldn't be long before Poppy left her little flat at her parent's pub and moved in permanently with Tom.

As predicted, as soon as the horses had been fed, watered and turned out, the front door swung open to Tom's welcoming committee. Harry stood back as Mallie and Jewel tumbled over one another in their eagerness to greet Tom on his return. Poppy waited patiently for them to receive their fuss before he turned his attention to her, softly planting a kiss on her cheek, then headed inside.

"Hurry up, Harry," Poppy called out, as she ushered him inside. "Dinner's on the table!"

Harry felt the warmth of the fire as he took his place at the table. As Poppy served them all hearty plates of home-made cottage pie, he took a moment to survey the room. It was a marked improvement to how he'd left it. After all the problems Tom had told him about with the flood over Christmas, he'd certainly put a lot of work and effort into making it habitable again. And now with Poppy on the scene, he noticed the subtlety of feminine touches. The vase of flowers on the table, the flickering, scented candles dotted about, and freshly-baked cupcakes cooling on the wire rack. After the madness of Tom's return, Mallie and Jewel were snoozing in front of the fireplace, and he knew that Poppy was the reason Tom had made the decision to get himself a dog. Tom had been on about getting a dog ever since his collie passed away a few years ago. But no doubt he felt so swamped with responsibility ever since Harry left, he didn't think it fair to bring a dog into the mix. But now he had Poppy to help, and with Mallie to keep her company, Jewel was the perfect addition to their little budding family. Poppy seemed to have effortlessly transformed the brother's old bachelor pad into a welcoming home.

Harry zoned back into the conversation Tom and Poppy were having about their friends, Charlie and Eleanor. It would appear that over the two years he'd been away, a lot of changes had taken place in the village. Poppy's parents had taken over the village pub, Eleanor had inherited Brambleberry cottage, and Charlie, from London, had moved in with her. He had a lot to catch up on if he was going to submerge himself back into the village he'd grown up in.

Wait, what was that?

"Who's getting married?" he asked.

"Eleanor and Charlie, of course!" replied Poppy. "They're our friends who own the cottage that Tom stayed in when his house was flooded. And they're having their wedding reception here!"

"All hands on deck when the time comes," chimed in Tom. "Especially as Rupert will no doubt be in attendance!"

Harry caught the look Tom gave Poppy before they both burst out laughing. *Who the hell is Rupert?*

Poppy quickly filled him in, explaining that Rupert was in fact Eleanor's miniature donkey, who lived in her house! "He's utterly adorable, you'll love him!"

"He's an absolute menace!" said Tom.

And then Poppy went on to inform him that the new horse who'd arrived belonged to Isobel, Charlie's long-lost daughter, who'd brought him all the way over from America

"There's a story there, for sure," she finished, her voice filled with curiosity.

Well, he thought, as he tucked into Poppy's apple crumble with cream, *who needs to travel halfway across the world for adventure when the gossip seems to be spreading thick and fast in his pokey little village of home!*

Isobel

Isobel sipped her mug of tea, took a huge bite of her apple pastry, then flicked her eyes out of the kitchen window to see Eleanor, wearing her bright yellow wellington boots, and still in her fluffy purple dressing gown, tending to her new chickens in the garden. Rupert, who was never one to miss out, was busy tucking into a slice of hay, no doubt as a distraction after yesterday's mischief of trying to steal the chicken feed. Isobel smiled to herself. Eleanor really was the quirkiest, yet most lovable person she'd ever met.

Eleanor caught her eye, smiled broadly, then made her way back into the house. Isobel busied herself making Eleanor a cup of tea whilst Eleanor chatted away about her new feathery friends, a present from Charlie two weeks ago. As she watched Eleanor tuck into a plum pastry, then brush the flaky crumbs off her dressing gown, she wondered why she'd ever felt so anxious about telling both Eleanor and her father about her current predicament.

The night of her arrival, it had all come tumbling out, and in between her blubbering sobs, Eleanor had patted her back, and her father had made copious amounts of cups of tea. Neither of them judged, or pried; they'd just quietly listened. They'd talked long into the night, and both of them had welcomed her, with open arms, to stay with them for as long as she needed. Eleanor had even offered her the cottage next door now that Tom's house was all ship shape again and he was back living at his stables.

Rupert let himself in through his oversized cat flap, which Eleanor affectionately called his 'donkey door', and immediately eyed up the Danish pastry on the table.

"Absolutely not, you little monster!" said Eleanor affectionately, "you've already pinched one this morning, that one's for Charlie."

Isobel giggled to herself as Rupert nonchalantly sauntered off into the sitting room after being chastised. She thought how quickly she'd adjusted to having a donkey living inside a house. Meeting him on the stair way or seeing him snoozing on the sitting room floor was now her new normal!

"Before I forget," said Eleanor, "these are for you." She handed over the keys for the cottage next door.

"Are you sure?" asked Isobel. "Won't you miss out on holiday lets if I stay there instead of here?"

"You're more important that any holiday let! I can't tell you how excited Charlie and I are that you've chosen to stay with us for the next couple of months. It's only right you have your own space, so you can come and go as you please without us old busybodies being in your way!"

Isobel accepted the key gracefully, knowing it was futile to argue. Both her father and Eleanor had been adamant about her having the cottage next door when the idea first arose, and deep down, Isobel was grateful. She needed the privacy to think, and to plan for her new future.

"Now," she said, beaming at Eleanor, "you'd better get ready! We've got lots to do this morning!"

Isobel could be just as adamant at Eleanor, she reasoned to herself whilst she tapped her fingers on the kitchen side waiting for Eleanor to get dressed. One thing she'd learnt in a very short period of time was that Eleanor was the easiest going, least materialistic person she'd ever met. The only things she was interested in were Charlie, Rupert, her artwork, her home, and now Isobel. She and her father had held a somewhat sneaky conversation without Eleanor a few days ago. He was desperate for their wedding to be special, and for Eleanor to be completely and utterly spoiled. His many years of fast-paced, high-achieving work had rewarded him with a more than comfortable early retirement, and he had every intention of spending that money on Eleanor, if only she'd let him. Isobel was now learning how hard it was to spoil someone who felt utterly content wearing five-year-old comfortable jeans with trusty, worn-out boots, and whose happiness sprung from romping around the countryside with her little donkey at her side. Her father had lucked in when she'd mentioned how lovely the garden would look with a few hens pecking around creating the perfect country garden scene, a scene that she could re-create in watercolour to add to her thriving little art business. Well, he'd jumped on that idea in a flash, and now he got to enjoy watching Eleanor enjoying her perfect garden view every day. Chickens, however, did not help with the wedding situation. And this is where Isobel had offered her services. Today, Isobel was taking the bride to be to the local town to organise manicures, pedicures and hair appointments for Eleanor, Poppy, herself, and Eleanor's good friend Tilda, for the day before the wedding. Browsing, and with a bit of luck, some shopping, would follow, and then the typical tea and cake would finish off their girly day. Isobel was very much looking forward to it. A day focused on someone else, rather than wallowing in self-induced pity, and self-doubt was exactly what she needed.

Four hours later, Isobel watched Eleanor let herself into Brambleberry Cottage carrying one little bag. Their day had been a success! Eleanor had allowed herself to be swept up in Isobel's excitement, gaining ideas for the style of dress she liked, purchasing some beautiful daisy earrings for her big day, and willingly agreeing to book everything Isobel suggested for their girls pre-wedding pamper day. Isobel couldn't wait to tell her father! But that would have to wait until this evening. He'd decided to join Tom, Poppy and Harry for their trip to the horse sales, so for now, Isobel had a spare few hours to spend with Christopher.

The yard was perfectly quiet when she arrived. With Cassie, Tom's riding instructor, out on a hack with clients, Isobel revelled in having the place to herself. Christopher lazily trotted over to the paddock gate as soon as he spotted her. His welcoming nicker hastened her step, and in moments, she felt his warm breath on her ear as she embraced him.

As she meticulously groomed him from head to toe, she eyed up the generous sized sand school, with jump poles neatly stacked in the corner.

"What do you think?" she asked her horse. "Shall we play jumping today?"

Christopher snuffled her hand, which she chose to take as a solid yes from her horse.

Christopher busied himself investigating his new school whilst Isobel huffed and puffed dragging the jump wings and poles around to set up a suitable course of various sized jumps. Dusting herself off, she stood back to admire her handy work, then looked over to Christopher. "Let's play!"

Isobel began their warmup, and Christopher trotted keenly around the school, his ears pricked, eagerly awaiting his cues. She could feel his excitement building when she asked him to canter a lap around the school. Changing rein effortlessly, he continued to canter, waiting patiently for her to start the game. Isobel immediately felt his power build when she pointed him at the smallest jump, and with seemingly no effort at all, they glided over the three-foot jump.

"Too easy for you, is it?" she asked him out loud. "That was just the practise one!"

Around again they went, with Christopher taking the small jump in his stride, but this time, she continued with the course. Next, he sailed, foot perfect, over her four foot, three jump vertical combination.

"Still too easy?" she asked.

Christopher snorted, picking up the pace, eager to continue with their game.

"Ok, ok, we'll do them all this time!"

And with that, she pushed him forward, little jump, combination, and then the five-foot double oxer, which Christopher hungrily gobbled up in his stride. Laughing at her horse, and lost in her own world of Christopher, she powered on and after cantering around the school again, she repeated her little course. After they'd landed the double oxer for a third time, she noticed two vehicles towing horse boxes trundling up the drive.

"Time's up, buddy," she announced, not wanting to be in the way of whatever was about to be going on. She reached down to wrap her arms around Christopher in praise for his hard work over the enjoyable hour they shared, then swinging her leg over to dismount, she heard her name being called. Whipping her head around, she saw her father letting himself into the sand school.

"Dad!" she called out in surprise. Then catching his eye, she said happily, "I have so much to tell you!"

Harry

Harry wiggled his fingers then flexed his wrist. It felt good to finally have his plaster cast removed. Stepping away from the hospital, he headed towards his Land Rover, pleased with the news that he was now properly healed. He'd had the usual chastising for continuing to ride whilst wearing his cast, and when he asked the doctor how he knew, the doctor just pointed at his hat. Cowboy hats were common work attire in the Australian outback, and he'd soon grown accustomed to wearing one, but back in Cornwall, he rather stuck out like a sore thumb for the horse rider and trainer that he was. But bollocking aside, the doctor had deemed him good to go, and he couldn't wait to get started.

His trip to the horse sales last weekend had been rather fruitful, and now, chillaxing in a paddock at home were three unbacked three-year-olds, and one eleven-year-old gelding claiming to be the perfect gentleman school master. For the price Charlie paid for him, he'd better be, but Charlie had asked him to put him through his paces just to make super sure he was safe for Eleanor to ride. He'd been very clear about the fact that Eleanor was a nervous rider, but he wanted the horse to be enjoyed by them both and for that to happen, he was more than happy to pay a pretty penny for the privilege. Charlie had also assured him that he was not asking for a favour; he would pay the going rate, making him Harry's first client.

Driving home, Harry soaked up the lushness that was Cornwall's Garden of Eden. The rolling hills of green, dotted with plump cows grazing and ewes nursing their newly born spring lambs filled him with positivity for the new beginnings ahead of him. He wound down his window and inhaled the crisp fresh air; It was a far cry from the dusty, all-consuming heat of the outback.

His phone pinged, alerting him to a new message. In a split second he heard his brothers voice asking him to find him on the yard as soon as he got home - he had something he needed to discuss with him.

Harry replayed the message, but his brother's steady, calm voice gave nothing away. Panic swiftly replaced his budding positivity as his mind whirled into overdrive as to what his brother wanted to talk about. *Good news? Bad news? Have I done something wrong?* He tried to reason with himself that Tom had accepted him back. He'd encouraged him to buy the youngsters. If he was going to boot him out, surely he wouldn't have done that? Harry knew it was the guilt that fuelled these insecurities; a message from Tom before he'd left wouldn't have summoned the chronic anxiety instilled in him now. And he knew he wouldn't have even rushed back to investigate. He'd have just bumped into him at some point during the day for a casual chit chat. But now, he felt their relaxed brotherly relationship was in tatters, and he only had himself to blame. Consumed in a cloud of trepidation, Harry directed his Land Rover down Hill Valley Stables driveway.

Harry found Tom in his office. He could tell immediately that he was flustered, then being asked to close the door behind him filled him with dread. *This can't be good...*

Awkward small talk filled the small office as the brothers discussed Harry's hospital appointment. Harry couldn't bear it. "For the love of God, Tom, just spit it out! What do you want to talk about?"

"Poppy," blurted out his brother.

"Ok," replied Harry cautiously, trying to understand what had got Tom so ruffled.

It took a while, but as Tom blundered his way through explaining his feelings for Poppy and his relief that Harry had returned home, Harry began to piece the jigsaw puzzle pieces that were his brother's mind together.

"I'll go," said Harry.

"What?"

"You want to ask Poppy to move in with you, but with me now home, three's a crowd, and you want me to go. I understand Tom. Poppy's wonderful, and you don't owe me anything." Harry knew this day would come; he had just hoped he would have had longer to get himself back on his feet. It was enough, though, that Tom had welcomed him back and allowed him to set up his own business from the stables. He wasn't going to push his luck.

"You misunderstand me, Harry."

Harry stayed quiet and listened whilst his brother explained that he was desperate for Harry to stay. How he wanted to build the business and now that Harry was home, they could continue their plan of being a horse training and riding school operation, and the relief that he could share the responsibility with his brother again. And with that, he could actually have some time to spend with Poppy, to spoil her and take her away every now and again.

Harry felt his anxiety slipping away as his brother talked. Tom was asking for help, and Harry couldn't think of a better way to start proving to his brother how much he wanted the second chance he was being offered. And with that, the god forsaken guilt that he carried with him every single day, might ease, just a little, if he could step up and help.

"I'm happy to hold the fort whenever you'd like a weekend away with Poppy."

"Really?" replied Tom, "I don't want to put too much pressure on you too soon."

Harry assured him that he was more than willing to keep everything ticking over, and he'd have the reliable Cassie keeping him in line the whole time! Tom agreed that his hard-working right-hand woman would most definitely be the one running the show!

Harry noticed a calmness settle over his brother, and he wanted to keep it that way. "I'll find somewhere else to live," he said quietly.

"Actually, I had an idea about that. What if we put a log cabin up on the other side of the yard? That way we would both be on site but not in each other's pockets."

Harry's heart thumped beneath his chest. That had been their plan when they took over the stables, they'd even flipped a coin to see who'd get the house and who'd get the cabin. Harry had won the cabin, and now, it would seem that Tom hadn't forgotten. But Harry wondered where he would now stand for funding their project. Before the coin toss, they'd discussed at length the cost of the cabin, against the cost of the repairs and modernisation of the main house. It had been agreed that the loan would cover the cost of the repairs and the cabin, but whoever got the cabin covered the cost of the groundwork and foundations. Harry did some quick calculations in his head. If he lived off baked beans on toast until the sale of his three-year-old horses and coupled this with the small savings he'd squirreled away from his work in Australia, he might just about afford it.

"I stand by our agreement, if you do?" said Tom, as if he was reading Harry's mind. "I'll re-coup the money I've had to shell out on all the repairs for the house after the flooding situation, you pay for the foundations, and we repay the loan together."

Harry was up on his feet, grasping his brother's hand in his, firmly shaking on their old plan becoming their new plan.

An hour later Harry was putting Mr Guiness, Charlie's new horse, through his paces. So far, the fifteen hand, stocky coloured cob was proving to be the perfect gentleman. Harry hadn't met Eleanor yet but from what Charlie and Poppy had told him about her, she'd be in safe hands with Mr Guiness. The plucky little cob behaved impeccably while being groomed and tacked up, and Harry knew his kind a mile off. If Eleanor wanted to lavish him with hugs and kisses whilst grooming him, well, Mr Guiness was definitely the type to stand for hours to be adored! He had three nice paces and eagerly popped a little jump. Harry dismounted and led the cob out of the school and back onto the yard. Tomorrow, he'd see if his manners were just as good out on a hack.

The beautiful warmblood was idling at the paddock gateway, watching curiously as Harry went about his business untacking and grooming Mr Guiness. Harry couldn't help but admire him. His breeding was no doubt top notch, and the way he'd seen Charlie's daughter jump him, so cleanly, and so effortlessly, together, they had been like poetry in motion. He looked out for them whenever he passed the yard, eager to see them in action again, but so far, he'd been out of luck. The constant hubbub of Charlie and Eleanor's wedding forever being discussed in the background reminded him that Isobel was most likely being kept busy with all the preparations.

After stealing one last glance over the majestic horse, he turned his attention back to Mr Guiness. "Come along, old chap," he said to the horse, leading him over to his own paddock. "I've got lots to do," he continued, as he pointed at his other horses. Fuelled with motivation for his log cabin, he was keen to get to work.

Isobel

Isobel's day hadn't started quite as she planned. After learning about her father's purchase of Mr Guiness, she was now deeply committed to helping him keep the secret until his big reveal on the day of the wedding. Harry, Tom's brother, who so far she'd only seen from a distance, was keen for Mr Guiness to meet Rupert and find out if Charlie's final request of being able to take them out together would be a possibility. The scene conjured in her mind of Eleanor and her father, out and about in the Cornish countryside with their horse and mischief making miniature donkey made her feel all warm and fuzzy inside; she was determined to help that happen.

However, a panic-stricken phone call from Tilda, owner of the local craft and bookshop, and one of Eleanor's dearest friends, put a spanner in the works. At least the kerfuffle of Eleanor hurrying out of the door, with Isobel in tow, pushed aside any worries of Eleanor asking why Charlie might want to take Rupert for a walk without her, enabling the secret to be kept for now.

Tilda's bookshop was as traditional Cornish country village style as you could get. Beautiful hanging baskets bursting with the whites and purples of early springtime flowers hung elegantly against the backdrop of typical Cornish stone. And stepping inside, Isobel could almost hear the gasps and shrieks of delight that any American would make on entering such a quaint English delight. She smiled to herself, thinking back to how many lovely comments she'd had over her English accent and little British quirks when she was living in New York.

It transpired that Tilda's flustered phone call was the result of new bookkeeping software uploaded onto her computer.

"He promised me that it would make life easier. He said it was the most efficient way to keep on top of everything and the easiest system to use," Tilda babbled, trying to hold back her tears of frustration as she explained her phone call with a salesman last week. "But I've lost all this year's invoices, I have no idea how to input my weekly sales and now I don't know what to do. It's a disaster!"

Isobel held back when Eleanor swooped into the rescue, wrapped her arms around her friend, then calmly led her into the back kitchen suggesting a cup of tea was very much needed.

"Would you mind if a take a look?" Isobel called out. She could feel her brain waking up as her eyes scanned the computer.

"Please do," replied Tilda, "I'll take any help I can get."

Within minutes, Isobel had found the 'lost' invoices and updated the sales records. And she agreed with the salesman; it was an efficient, up to-date bookkeeping system. As she familiarised herself with the system, she couldn't help herself. Numbers were what she did, and she found some small errors with Tilda's work. And the system was so easy to use that her quick mind picked out glaringly obvious ways that Tilda could spend money more efficiently, save money, and reduce her tax payments.

Once Tilda regained her composure, Isobel slowly talked her through the new computer system, and credit to Tilda, she grasped it quite quickly. Isobel didn't want to be rude, but equally, she knew exactly what needed to be done to maximise profits, and she wanted to help. As subtly as she could, she pointed out little changes Tilda could make to run her business more efficiently, and to her delight, Tilda was eager to listen and willingly took down notes as Isobel explained her ideas.

An hour later, Isobel was reaping her reward. Tilda had left Eleanor to put the kettle on whilst she popped out to the bakery to buy treats, and now, Isobel was tucking in to a freshly baked cream and jam donut, whilst being showered in praise from both Tilda and Eleanor. Isobel felt the buzz alone from activating her work brain after such a long break was reward enough, but she happily munched away, quietly pleased that she'd made a difference to Tilda's little business. And the appreciation Tilda showed her was for more personal and enjoyable than the multi-million dollar, faceless corporate companies she was used to working for.

Cocooned in Tilda's tiny kitchen at the back of her shop, Isobel settled into her chair as Eleanor and Tilda turned their conversation to village news, and what Isobel could only call a good old gossip! She soon found out that nothing went on in the little village of Willowdown without Tilda knowing about it! They chatted away about baking a cake for someone's husband who'd just come out of hospital, and debated what was better, a lasagne or a cottage pie, to take to the mum in the village who'd just had baby number three. Then the conversation turned to poor old Harry.

Harry? Isn't he the cowboy at the yard?

Isobel's ears pricked at the thought of almost knowing one of the characters from Eleanor and Tilda's gossip session. It transpired that he'd returned from a stint in Australia at the same time Isobel had moved Christopher to Hill Valley Stables. She also learned that his reason for being in Australia was because of a blond haired, perfectly tanned Australian beauty. But all wasn't as it seemed once he'd got there. Apparently, Harry told Tom, who'd told Poppy, who'd told her mum...*Blimey,* thought Isobel, trying to keep up! That said blond beauty had left a broken-hearted boyfriend back in Australia, and after only a few months of Harry being there, rekindled with the ex.

"You couldn't make it up!" said Tilda. And in typical Tilda style, as the one who was most protective over all her fellow Willowdown residents, she continued, "We must look after Harry whilst he settles in back home." And Eleanor nodded in firm agreement.

Isobel and Eleanor found Charlie sitting at the kitchen table sharing an apple with Rupert when they returned to Brambleberry Cottage. The conspiratory wink her father gave her told her that all had gone well with Mr Guiness and Rupert. Declining her father's offer for a trip out to lunch at the village pub due to the two cream donuts she'd consumed at Tilda's, she left Eleanor to fill him in about their morning at Tilda's and headed off to the yard.

Mallie and Jewel bowled into her as soon as she stepped out of her car. Their excited yips and licky dog kisses caused her to burst out laughing as she fussed and cuddled them in return. She found Poppy on the yard, grooming her horse, Daphne. *Perfect!* She was keen to ask Poppy directions for the woodland ride her father had mentioned the other day.

Isobel listened intently and tried to follow as best she could, but left at the big tree, down a bit, take the right by the metal gate...not the wooden gate, was a little bit confusing!

"I'll take you," said a voice from inside the tack room.

Isobel and Poppy whipped round to see Harry carrying Billy's saddle and bridle.

"Tom's got a full packed day with clients and asked me to exercise Billy for him. We can go the woodland route if you'd like to join us?"

"Oh, great," said Poppy enthusiastically.

A funny feeling formed in the pit of Isobel's belly. It was a strange combination of both mortification and guilt by suddenly being thrust into Harry's company, the memories swirling around her mind from the earlier conversation with Tilda about his time in Australia. Finding herself in his presence changed him from a somewhat fictional character of conversation to a real-life person, bringing with it the feeling that she'd now inadvertently intruded on his privacy. He was a stranger, yet unbeknown to him, she knew details of his private life that she shouldn't. It didn't sit right with her, and an uncomfortable warmth spread to her cheeks. She reached out to stroke Daphne, grateful the gentle horse was standing between them, in the hope of shielding her embarrassment from Harry.

"Isobel?" said Poppy.

Hearing her name puncture through the awkward silence she'd unwittingly created, Isobel quickly pulled herself together.

"Yes, thank you," she replied, "I'll just get Christopher ready."

She scuttled off to bring Christopher in from the field, hoping she could get her emotions under control by the time she climbed into the saddle.

Harry

It had been a split second's decision to invite Isobel to go riding with him. It was slightly selfish on his part if truth be told, because he'd been waiting for the opportunity to see the majestic warmblood in action again. He knew it would be a good ride, because Christopher was the only other horse on the yard in the same league as Billy. And it wasn't very often Tom allowed anyone near his pride and joy, let alone allowed anyone to ride him, so in Harry's mind, luck had been on his side. However, ten minutes into the ride, Harry was marginally regretting his idea, because Isobel had hardly spoken a word. Rather than listen to the deafening silence between them, he chose to focus on the tweeting birds singing their springtime song, the gentle flow of the brook which ran parallel to the rugged track, and in the distance, the bleat of the little lambs calling for their mothers. As he tuned into the nature all around him, he found himself feeling at peace as he plodded along on his brother's horse. So much so, that he actively gave a little jump of surprise when Isobel's voice rang out like a church bell in the stillness of the air. He had almost forgotten she was with him.

"Harry, wait," called out Isobel. "Can we stop for a moment please?"

"Is everything all right?" he asked, cursing himself for not taking better care of his companion.

"Not really, no," she replied, not quite meeting his eye. "You see, the thing is..."

He rolled his eyes over Christopher, but couldn't see anything wrong with him, so he waited, curiously, for her to finish her sentence.

"The problem with a small village is that everyone seems to know everyone's business."

Not where I thought this was going...

"And we are virtually strangers, yet I happen to know an awful lot about you, and well," she finally raised her eyes to meet his. "Well, that doesn't seem right."

What does she know? But he didn't have time to ponder on it because Isobel then launched into a soliloquy about how her own life was skyrocketing wildly off track. She'd burst into tears in front of her boss before promptly packing in the most perfect job in New York that she'd dreamed of ever since studying for her A Levels. She'd then flown herself and Christopher half way across the world, and somehow ended up on her estranged father's doorstep, with no future plan, and no job in sight.

"Phew," she laughed nervously, "Now we're on an even footing! I just can't stand dishonesty! We can carry on with the ride now if you like?"

Harry nodded at her and asked Billy to walk on, and the horses fell into step side by side. His mind whizzed with the influx of information he'd just received at the speed of light. Finally finding his tongue, he asked what it was exactly she knew about him.

"Oh, that," she said casually, as if she'd almost forgotten how her overflow of information had come about. "That you went to Australia because of some tanned beauty but it all ended when you found out she was still in love with her ex-boyfriend, who she then got back with. You more or less got your heart broken and decided to come back to England."

Ouch... "Yes, that pretty much sums it up."

He wanted to be annoyed. He felt he ought to be cross that he was being so freely gossiped about, but in all honesty, he just felt relief. He was doing his best to put Australia and everything that had happened there behind him, so he figured that if everyone knew, well, it saved him the bother of explaining himself, and quite frankly, they'd soon grow bored of his pathetic antics and find someone else to talk about...that was village life for you. And he also noted how refreshing Isobel's open frankness was. After the consistent deceit and multitude of unspoken words with Adele, Isobel's bold honesty was a breath of fresh air.

Harry nudged Billy ahead of Christopher as they reached the end of the grassy track and stepped onto the single file path. He felt Billy's excitement quietly bubbling away inside him waiting for his cue to gather some speed and have some fun!

"Happy to pick up the pace?" he asked, twisting around in his saddle, to be met with Isobel's smile, so beautifully real as her blue eyes twinkled right back at him.

"Absolutely."

The eager horses were off. Billy knew the woodland routes well, and he paused only for a split second as Harry directed him left or right, each time the path forked, and he never faltered in his stride when he was presented with a fallen-down tree or stranded log sprawled across his way. Harry revelled in the horse's speed and agility, and he hoped that one day, he would be able to afford the luxury of such a wonderful horse for himself.

He could hear Christopher's thundering hooves close behind him;

he knew he'd be able to keep up! But the real test was nearing. He gently slowed Billy down to navigate the gateway signalling the border of the woodland, and the entrance to five wide open fields, just begging to be galloped across. Isobel trotted Christopher up alongside him, allowing a moment for the horses to catch their breath. Isobel's cheeks glowed a soft rose pink, causing him to notice how pretty she looked with a bit of colour, and a smile on her face. He hadn't realised until now that she usually looked rather pale and almost a little haunted, but after her gushing outburst of oversharing earlier on, it all made sense. It was understandable that she looked as if she'd been through the mill. *I'm not the only one picking up the pieces of my own mess*, he thought. And he decided in that very moment that he would make the effort to make sure she felt welcomed at the yard, and to make it clear to her that she had a friend in him, if she wanted.

"Are we going to race?" she asked playfully, gesturing to the far-reaching grassy fields.

She noted his quick nod and pushed her horse up a gear. The horses accelerated quickly, devouring the ground beneath them, galloping side by side. Christopher kept a steady pace alongside Billy, just like Harry thought he would. He knew Billy still had more in the tank, which he would have quite freely asked for had he been racing his brother! But today was not that day, and riding with Isobel rather than against her was a far more enjoyable reward.

The ride along the lanes back home was a far cry from the awkward silence at the start of their ride. It would seem that Isobel was quite the little chatterbox, now that the ice was broken between them, after she had confessed all about her past.

Christopher seemed to be her favourite topic of conversation, as did telling him the hilarious tales of what Rupert got up to, and how she felt sorry for Cassie as she'd heard that it was her who'd volunteered to look after the naughty little donkey at the wedding. She must have caught the confusion etched on his face as she moved on to explain that Rupert would indeed be part of the wedding party! Once they were on the topic of the wedding, she babbled on about lunch at the pub next weekend, reminding him that Charlie had very kindly included him on the pub lunch when he insisted that he must come to the wedding. He was not only the brother of Charlie's best friend, but the wedding reception was also being held at his stables, so it was only right for him to be there.

The yard was a hubbub of activity when they arrived. Cassie was leading a string of customers out on a hack, Tom was teaching a jumping lesson in the sand school, Poppy was in the office trying to get to grips with Tom's haphazard filing system in order to help him get on top of his never-ending paperwork, and Mallie and Jewel were rooting out mice in the hay barn. The busyness of the yard reminded Harry how much he loved to be a part of it all, but it did not leave much room for continuing any sort of conversation with Isobel. She thanked him for inviting her and Christopher on his ride, then blended into the background of the yard effortlessly as she tended to her horse.

Much later that evening, Harry took himself to the paddock where his youngsters grazed, to watch the pinks and yellows trailing the sky and the burnt orange sun slowly drifting away, in solitude.

Today's been a good day. The best day I've had in a very long time. He thought back to Isobel, and how refreshing he found her honesty, and how enthusiastic she'd been chatting about her horse, and her father's upcoming nuptials, even with her own life being in a complete muddle right now. He pictured her sparkling blue eyes and found himself counting the days out on his fingers until the pub lunch. He was very much looking forward to seeing Isobel again.

Isobel

It was five o'clock in the morning and Isobel, along with her father and Eleanor, were heading home under a clear night sky, their warm breath clouding the early springtime chilly air with each step they took. Rupert, looking the picture of innocence, trotted elegantly at Eleanor's side, very much enjoying his impromptu family walk. Eleanor, however, did not look as if she was enjoying it quite so much. Isobel couldn't help but chuckle as Eleanor did her best to scold the little donkey, knowing full well that he wouldn't take a blind bit of notice!

Today's mischief had come to light when Rupert, having taken himself to the pub when everyone at Brambleberry Cottage was snoozing the night away, was caught red handed munching his way through the delicious flower garden. He'd scared the life out of Poppy's parents with all his banging and crashing around in their garden. They'd been convinced it was an intruder, but on realising who the culprit was, and accepting that this was just village life, the ever-amiable pub landlady contacted Eleanor in the wee hours to see if she could please come and retrieve him before her beer garden was completely emptied of all the pretty flowers!

Isobel felt for Eleanor. Of all the days he could choose to massacre the pub flowers, it had to be the same day she'd booked a table at the pub...in the garden, no less, so that Rupert, Mallie and Jewel could be included in the pre wedding catchup with her friends over a bite to eat...*You couldn't make it up!*

The moonlit party arrived at Brambleberry Cottage, Eleanor hugged Isobel in thanks for all her help with the rescue mission, then took her naughty donkey inside, stating it was time for him to think about what he'd done whilst she set about making yet another apology card on his behalf. Her father smiled wryly.

"Never a dull moment around here!" he said, before following his future wife inside.

No, Isobel thought, *there certainly isn't!*

It was too late to go back to bed, and with her only appointment in the diary being the pub lunch later that day, she decided that she'd spend her unexpected extra time at the yard, with Christopher.

Arriving at the yard, the sky above her was smoky blue, signalling that dawn was doing her best to push through the darkness of the night and bring with her the new day. Christopher greeted her at the paddock gateway, surprised, yet eager to see her at this unusually early hour. She led him into his stable, and being in no hurry at all, set about grooming him thoroughly from the tip of his nose to the tip of his tail. She wound the brush in rhythmical circles over his body, and when she reached his scratchy spots, she felt him lean into the pressure, assuring her that he was enjoying his morning pamper session just as much as she was.

Isobel's peaceful solitude was interrupted when she heard iron-clad hooves walking over the concrete yard, and the gentle whispers of whoever was leading the horse. Straining her ears, she heard the click of a gate, then the soft thud as the horse's hooves hit the sand in the school, signalling to her that whoever was out there was also enjoying the privacy and solitude the early morning had to offer.

Peeking out of the stable, she saw one of Harry's youngsters floating in circles around him in the school. She watched him gently praise the horse, then send him around the other way. A very curious Christopher joined her at the door, and together, they watched the man in a cowboy hat and his horse. Time for Isobel felt inconsequential as she watched Harry slowly but surely build the horse's confidence until he saddled the horse, put his foot in the stirrup, effortlessly swing his leg over, and comfortably sat in the saddle. The horse didn't seem to so much as blink at his friend transitioning from being next to him, to now sitting on his back. Isobel had never seen anything like it, and she watched, transfixed, as the horse carefully balanced its new rider, before listening to Harry's cue and tentatively walking on. Harry dismounted, praised the horse and headed back to the sand school gate just as the sun cast her yellow rays, alerting the world that morning had arrived.

Isobel ducked back into her stable, her mind whizzing in overdrive. She'd just witnessed the most intimate connection between horse and rider, to the point where she felt like she'd intruded yet again into Harry's private life... *What is wrong with me!* And at the same time, she revisited the guilt she felt on hearing about his romantic disaster in Australia, and again, the guilt when she turned up on her father's doorstep without fully disclosing her current situation. It didn't sit right with her. She heard the horse's hooves hitting the hard surface of the yard. *Here we go...*

"Hi Harry," she said, revealing herself at the stable door. He looked right at her, the rising sun failing to hide the colour running to his cheeks.

"Looks like we both fancied some quiet time on the yard this morning," she ploughed on, filling the ever-growing silence between them. Her confidence beginning to crumble, she decided to cut to the chase. "I'm sorry if you feel like I've imposed on your training time, it really was wonderful to watch you back the youngster..." Her voice trailed off.

"Thank you," was all he replied, as he led the horse over to the other end of the yard.

Isobel hugged her horse. "At least I've got you," she said, kissing his nose, "now let's go riding before we cause any more trouble around here!"

***

Isobel was quietly pleased when Eleanor complimented her on her outfit. She'd wanted to make the effort for Eleanor, to let her know that she was in full support of her marrying her father, and the pre-wedding get-together was just the place to do that. Her careful choice of pairing her green woollen dress with her brown boots, tweed coat and cream scarf seemed to have done the trick.

Isobel was doing her very best to focus. This was her father and Eleanor's moment, after all. But wafts of Harry's citrus infused aftershave kept distracting her. *Maybe I've romanticised his training session too much? Maybe it's because he always wears that cowboy hat...and what girl doesn't like a cowboy! Stop it Isobel, concentrate...* It had been a very long time since Isobel had harboured any flirtatious feelings for anyone. So long, in fact, that it had taken her the first hour of the lunch date to realise what they were, and now her anxiety was skyrocketing in fear that anyone around the table would know her innermost thoughts. And anyway, after this morning's faux pas with Harry, she doubted very much he even liked her right now, let alone anything else.

"Isobel?" said Eleanor, with questioning eyes, pulling her back into the present conversation. "Tilda was just saying..."

Isobel looked up to find not only Eleanor, but her dad, Tom, Poppy, Tilda and Harry all staring back at her.

But before she had chance to reply, Tilda launched in to how marvellous she thought Isobel was, and how she hoped she didn't mind, but she'd given her phone number out to some of her friends who would love some help with their own accounts.

"I also told them there would be a price!" she said rather sternly. "A clever girl like you, with a first class degree from Cambridge no less, should not be taken advantage of. I hope you don't mind?"

Isobel looked at Tilda. *How could I mind!* she thought. Tilda had done nothing but welcome her warmly to the village, praise her to anyone who'd listen, and pretty much made herself available to be a firm friend should Isobel like to take her up on it. She really did like her, and if it meant helping a few of her friends, then it really was a small price to pay for all the kindness Tilda had shown her.

"Of course not, Tilda, I'm happy to help," Isobel said, and she was rewarded with a beaming smile from Tilda.

"A first class degree from Cambridge?" said Harry quietly once the conversation had turned back to the wedding.

Isobel felt herself blush at the first chance that had arisen over lunch to speak directly to Harry. "Yes," she replied softly.

"I barely scraped through secondary school. I couldn't wait to leave so I could spend all my time with the horses," confessed Harry. "And in the spirit of your much-loved honesty," he said with a playful tone, "don't feel bad about watching me back the youngster, because I very much enjoyed watching you jumping the other day when we came home from the horse sales. So, are we even now?"

Isobel's anxiety ebbed away as she nodded her agreement. Over the course of the lunch, she and Harry chatted effortlessly whenever the chance arose. As the lunch party prepared to depart, Harry called her over.

"I'm going to meet a potential client and her horse in a couple of days, you'd be welcome to come with me?"

"Yes, please," she replied, just as Rupert came blundering between them, his lead rope trailing behind, having escaped poor Eleanor again. His antics causing raucous laughter amongst not only their own party, but all the other pub goers too, as he beelined for the flower beds, enjoying his fleeting moment of freedom before the ever-patient Eleanor retrieved him and firmly told him it was time to go home.

Harry

Harry was on his way to meet the new client, with Isobel sitting quietly next to him in the passenger seat of his Land Rover. Since his return, he'd taken the time to reach out to old friends and acquaintances, alerting them that he'd returned from his travels and was back in the horse training business. His previous reputation seemed to hold him in good stead, as did the knowledge that although he'd been away, training horses had still been his trade when in Australia. And so, slowly but surely, old clients were beginning to learn of his return, and potential new clients were finding out about his existence and were reaching out to him.

"This is it," said Isobel, pointing to the sign, 'Tilby Stables.'

Pulling onto the yard, Harry found two women, a mother and young adult daughter duo, eagerly waiting for him. After initial introductions were completed, they took Harry and Isobel to see the horse in question. The sixteen-hand dapple grey warmblood was just as beautiful as they'd described, and Harry listened quietly as the daughter tacked him up and the mother explained about the accident at her daughter's last show.

"The vet said he wasn't injured at all, and that he's perfectly fine to be working again, but he's refusing jumps and spooking in the ring, which is totally out of character," said the mother.

The placid horse followed his mistress out of the stable and into the sand school. He stood politely for her to mount, then eagerly followed her cues for his warmup. But when faced with a jump, he slammed his breaks on, reversed, then cantered around the jump.

Harry had seen enough. He asked her to dismount, swung his own leg over the horse, and settled himself into the saddle. He worked the horse around the school, and the beautiful show jumper transitioned fluently between his three paces. He pointed him at the jump, and he sailed over, foot perfect. Harry cantered him around the school, then tried another jump, slightly bigger this time, and not even a moment's hesitation from his mount. The horse knew his job and performed it excellently. Harry felt a little buzz as they soared over another jump, at the privilege to be riding such a master of his profession. There was absolutely nothing wrong with him, and now he'd have to tell the slightly overbearing mother that the problem lay with his rider. He slowed the horse and walked over to his trio of spectators, and just as he was trying to find the words to be as polite as possible, the daughter spoke out.

"It's me, isn't it?"

"Maybe the accident has knocked your confidence," he replied kindly, noticing she was trying to hold back her tears.

She nodded back at him. He could feel her almost willing him to fix her on the spot, but that was something he couldn't do.

Then she girl turned to Isobel. "Would you ride him for me?"

"I'm not a horse trainer!" replied Isobel.

"That's the whole point. Of course, Harry can ride him, that's his job! But maybe if I could see just a normal person ride him, then it might boost my confidence, what do you think?" she said, looking at Isobel. "And you did say that you jumped your own warmblood, didn't you?"

Harry didn't like where this conversation was going, and he certainly didn't want Isobel to feel under any pressure from Little Miss Doe Eyes... honestly, the cheek of some people.

"I'm afraid Isobel is only here to watch," he told the daughter.

"It's ok," chimed in Isobel. "I'd love to ride him."

And before anyone could say anything else, she'd put on the daughter's hat, mounted the horse, and was now confidently cantering him around the school. Harry's heart skipped a beat watching Isobel and the magnificent grey soar over the first jump. It was the same all-encompassing feeling that enveloped him when he saw her jump Christopher. He couldn't put his finger on it, he couldn't put it into words, but his whole being felt at peace as he watched her ride.

"I've got no excuse now!" said the daughter, after witnessing Isobel's foot perfect round with her horse.

Harry spent the next hour building the daughter's confidence. He started with small cross poles, and slowly, as she regained her confidence and trust in her horse, their bond deepened and they became a jumping team once again. Harry left with a cheque in his pocket and a pair of very happy customers, and he knew he had Isobel to thank for it.

Driving home, Harry pulled over when they came across a bustling village pub.

"Lunch time," he announced. "My treat to say thank you for all your help today."

Isobel tried to swish his compliment away, muttering about how grateful she was that he'd invited her along and how much fun she'd had. But Harry wouldn't hear of it. He wanted to show her his appreciation, and he also wanted to do something nice for her, just because he could.

There was a warmth in the spring air, so they chose a table in the pretty pub garden where they could enjoy the view of two ducks bobbing around on the pond, enjoying the sunshine. Over lunch, they chatted contentedly about his customers that morning and the beautiful horse, which led them on to talking about Christopher. Harry loved how Isobel's eyes lit up whenever her beloved horse was mentioned, and how passionately she spoke about him. Harry was enjoying one of life's perfect moments, cocooned in the pub garden, the sunshine sparkling on the placid pond, and Isobel, her cheeks pink from laughing as she recalled Rupert's moonlight walk. And in a split second, his bubble of happiness burst like a balloon.

"I'll miss the little monster when I leave," said Isobel, affectionately.

Leaving? Where's she going?

He tried to keep his voice steady as he gently probed her statement. She reminded him that her father's wedding was now only a couple of weeks away, and once the big day itself had been and gone, her time would be up. Tom had very kindly agreed for Christopher to stay the full three months, and Eleanor had offered her holiday cottage until the wedding. She couldn't take advantage of everyone's kind nature for longer than that, and she also couldn't flounder around Cornwall indefinitely, no matter how much she was enjoying herself.

Harry felt a wave of disappointment flow right through him. He recalled their first ride together, when Isobel had massively overshared after hearing gossip about him. She'd told him then that she would be in Cornwall until the wedding, but he had forgotten, or deliberately chosen to ignore, that piece of information. He had no one to blame but himself for his unsettled feelings right now. He sensed the atmosphere between them simmer with potential awkwardness as she tailed off, no doubt due to his sudden fluctuation in mood. He checked himself quickly. It was not Isobel's fault he'd chosen to ignore the information she'd willingly given him. It was not Isobel's fault that looking out for her on the yard was now part of his daily routine, and nor was it her fault that there were flutters, deep in the pit of his belly if by chance, he got lucky and bumped into her whilst tending to Christopher. It dawned on him how he'd taken her being around for granted, and that he knew his home would always be Hill Valley Stables, but Isobel not being around anymore, well, it would certainly take the shine off his days.

He smiled up at her. He would be kind, and be her friend, just like she'd been to him. And he would support her new future; in whichever direction she chose to take it. He, of all people, knew how stressful life-changing decisions could be, and he would not take out his own disappointment on someone who already had more than enough plates to juggle.

A huge ice-cream Sunday, with whipped cream and a cherry on top, drifted past them as the waiter carried it over to its eager customer.

"Oh, gosh. Food envy!" he exclaimed to Isobel. "Fancy sharing one of those?"

He was rewarded with her adorable smile. "Oh, yes please!"

And at least for that moment, his world was right again.

Isobel

Isobel climbed into her car, turned back to wave at Mrs Walker, then drove five minutes out of the local town until she came across a layby. Turning her engine off, she took out her purse and counted the sixty pounds again. She'd been true to her word and agreed to help two of Tilda's friends with their accounts. Vivienne, from the laundrette, and Mrs Walker from the jewellery store. And she'd also agreed to meet with a fish and chip shop owner tomorrow. Tilda really did know everyone! Each meeting had lasted about an hour, and both customers had been thrilled with her work and her ideas for making their little businesses more profitable. Isobel had no idea what to charge, but Tilda had covered that too. She explained that she'd done her research and told everyone she passed Isobel's number onto that her fee was thirty pounds per hour. Initially, Isobel felt bad for even thinking about charging Tilda's friends. The work, for Isobel at least, was easy and straight forward, but she had very much enjoyed putting her brain into action again, and now, feeling the paper money between her fingers, she realised that it felt good to be earning a bit of pocket money after merrily draining her savings over the last two months.

Isobel checked her watch. It was time to put her pennies away and head to the yard. She'd promised her dad that she'd ride out with him and Mr Guiness, and she was looking forward to it. As her car trundled along the country lanes, she thought back to how much her life had changed ever since her father's out of the blue email landed in her inbox last summer. She mulled over all that had happened and waited. But the usual feeling of anxiety and panic didn't arrive.

Ok, I'll try again. She thought about her life in New York, her work and colleagues, and the huge monthly sum of money that was no longer entering her bank account. But the regret wasn't there. Instead, her mind wandered to Brambleberry Cottage, and how welcoming the little home was. She thought about the sense of easy comfortableness that enveloped both Brambleberry and The Cottage Next Door like a warm, cosy blanket. She thought about what her life had become in Willowdown village, how everyone smiled and waved at her, and how settled Christopher was at Hill Valley stables...and Harry. She felt herself blush, even in the privacy of her own car, at how her crush on the handsome cowboy was no doubt a large part of why she loved going to the stables so much. And how much she enjoyed the snippets she caught of him training the horses. It was only when the thought of having to leave the little world her father, and his friends had created for her in Cornwall that the anxiety began to kick in. She tried to squash the feelings instantly.

You can't live off fresh air and the charity of your father, Isobel, she told herself firmly. *Enough galloping around the countryside with the cowboy, and enough idling your time away eating cakes and drinking tea with Eleanor in her perfectly homey kitchen. As soon as I get home from the yard this evening, I'm making the plan.* And she nodded to herself in her rear-view mirror to seal the deal.

Arriving at the yard, she found her father and Harry standing next to a large caravan, chatting away. Before getting out of the car, she quickly checked her reflection in the mirror, smoothed her hair down and barred her teeth to check there were no remnants of the slice of home-made cake she'd been offered at Mrs Walker's house. All good...*I've really got to get a handle on this crush*, she thought, knowing full well that the state of her hair wouldn't have entered her head if it was just her father waiting for her.

She walked over to investigate the caravan situation. On seeing her, Harry openly announced that it was to be his new home! He ploughed on about how he felt Tom and Poppy needed their own space, and it would be a few months yet before he could afford a log cabin as his permanent residence, and so, his new home would be on wheels for now. Isobel privately noted how Harry had pushed past his heartache from Australia, brought himself home, picked himself up and marched on with life. He was starting small, with the help of his brother, and his friends spreading the word for his business, and now he was prepared to call a tin box on wheels his home and was proud of it to boot. And she felt a glimmer of pride for him. She knew exactly how hard it was to try and change your life's direction. And yet, in the same time that had passed since she and harry had come to Cornwall, she still seemed to be aimlessly treading water. But she wasn't going to let her negativity ruin Harry's moment, and she and her father gladly accepted the tour of Harry's new home...and she had to admit, it wasn't all that bad inside!

Later, Mr Guiness and Christopher plodded along side by side as Isobel listened to Charlie fill her in on all the last-minute wedding preparations. The familiar warm fuzzy feeling trickled through her, just like it always did, when she heard Charlie talking about Eleanor. She was so pleased he'd found happiness. Her parents' marriage might have been a disaster, but her mother was now very happily married to a man that adored her, and her father had finally found peace within himself, and had his beloved Eleanor. A smidge of jealousy tried to wiggle through her happy thoughts. *When will it be my turn? When will I find my happy ever after?* But she stamped it out as fast at it came, reminding herself that self-pity was not a pleasant rock to crawl under.

Charlie brought her back into the moment when he mentioned he'd been stopped by a gentleman in the bakery today, asking if Isobel was his daughter, and would she be able to take a look at his books. His hardware store in the neighbouring village had become stagnant and he was keen to discuss potential savings and ideas. Charlie had taken his number, with a promise to pass it on to Isobel.

"You're becoming quite popular around here, Isobel," he said, with a tinge of pride in his voice.

"That's all thanks to Tilda!" she laughed in reply. "And yes, I'd be happy to go through some business ideas with him. Thanks, Dad."

She knew her dad was hoping she'd offer up more information, most likely about what her long-term plans were, but as she didn't know herself yet, she had nothing to share. And he was far too polite to push for more. He might have been out of her life for nearly ten years, but she was most definitely his daughter, and he knew that she had to make the decision of how she was going to move forward with her life by herself, and in her own time.

Taking the pressure off both of them, her dad directed Mr Guiness off the country lane and down the track that headed to the moors.

"Shall we go running!" he asked.

It was still a new concept to Isobel that her father actually rode horses! Not once during her childhood had he shown any interest in them whatsoever. He was happy to pay for her lessons, and if work ever permitted, or her mother nagged hard enough, he'd watch her compete at pony club, but that was it. A tentative pat on the nose of whichever pony she was riding at the time was as much interest he'd ever shown. Now here he was, riding his own horse confidently next to her as if he'd been riding all his life! And he seemed so much happier for it. The dull, grey air that used to encompass him wherever he went was gone, as were the immaculate, personally tailored suits. His new attire comprised of jeans and boots. She'd even noticed that a button was missing from his shirt. Never in her life had she seen her father dressed in any way other than perfection, until his move to Cornwall. His sallow skin now glowed; his hands had a roughness to them from all the chores that came with horses...and a donkey! The only word she could think of to describe him now was content. And she hoped that one day, she would be lucky enough to find that too.

Her overactive mind settled when Christopher willingly picked up the pace and cantered steadily alongside Mr Guiness. Circling grey clouds filled the sky above them, but the threatening rain had not yet arrived, and even on a dull day, Isobel still managed to find a rugged beauty in the barren landscape of the moors, and a sense of peace within, even if it was only whilst riding.

Harry

Harry shook his new client's hand and promised him that the horse he had just spent the majority of his savings on for his teenage son was definitely fixable with the correct training. The unscrupulous dealer who'd sold the horse made Harry's blood boil, but that was the nature of buying a horse. Some sellers where honest and reliable, and others sold horses totally unsuitable for the prospective purchaser. The kind father had been well and truly taken for a ride, but after an hour with the horse, Harry concluded that the horse, who'd been sold to them as a school master but who had turned out to be a barely backed novice, showed promise. The horse had kind eyes, and a gentleness about him, if only he could be given the chance to learn the job he was being asked to do. Harry assured both father and son that he would be back in three days to ensure progress was being made, slowly but surely, for the young horse.

Harry climbed into his Land Rover and headed towards Willowdown village. It was completely the wrong direction for his next appointment of the day, but when he tentatively asked Isobel if she'd like to join him on a trip that he could only reveal to her once they were on their way, she'd jumped at the chance. He'd made the decision to carry on his friendship with Isobel as if she wasn't leaving. He knew she was, but when he thought about a world without Isobel in it, his heart ached, so he chose to ignore that little fact, and enjoy her company whilst he still had her. It seemed futile to cut off his nose to spite his face by backing away from her and the friendship he so enjoyed. He'd deal with his aching heart when she'd actually left. And his plan for today, he just knew Isobel would love, and he wanted to share it with her.

Isobel smiled and waved when she saw him pull up outside Brambleberry Cottage.

"So where are we going? Can you tell me now?" she said, curiosity etched across her face.

"Get in," he replied, laughing. "You have no patience!"

He'd barely driven for one minute before she asked again.

"Ok, ok," he said, relenting, passing over his phone.

He knew she wouldn't be able to wait until they arrived, so he'd taken a screenshot of the day's activity so she could find out for herself when she clicked on the photo album on his phone.

"Oh my gosh!" she squealed when the information was revealed to her. "You're getting a dog!"

A few days ago, alone in his caravan, Harry decided he needed a companion in his life. He couldn't afford the right horse yet and he didn't want a puppy. The yard was chaos enough with Jewel and Mallie! Plus, he didn't really have the time for puppy training with his ever-growing workload. But he wanted a companion. Someone who would be by his side in both the good times and the bad. Isobel and Christopher were proof that even if you decide to move back home from another country after chasing a dream, a companion animal came home with you. The pet of your choice stayed with you for life - unlike many humans, he mused. An adult dog was what he'd like. One that would be able to accompany him on his travels to different clients, and who would help mend his broken heart when Isobel left...not that he'd mention that part to Isobel, of course.

He'd spent the evening scrolling through local charities and rescue centres until he came upon an advert for a collie dog. She'd been given to the rescue centre, as her previous owners had claimed that her behaviour was disruptive in the home. The picture of the elegant collie caused him to stop and read her history. He realised straight away that the previous owners, who lived in a small-town house, with an even smaller garden and two young children, were the reason for the collie's misbehaviour. Collies were working dogs who needed exercise and stimulation - no wonder the poor dog dug up the garden and chewed all the furniture! The fit to bursting rescue centre had all but offered her to him on the spot when they found out that not only did he live on a farm, but that the collie would have constant company being able to go to work with him. They were more than accommodating in arranging a meeting, in the hope that he might be able to give the slightly troublesome collie a new home.

"How exciting," said Isobel. "I can't wait to meet her."

"Me too!" replied Harry as he drove into the rescue centre's carpark.

Bea, short for Beatrice, was a whirlwind of busyness when she burst through the door, eager to meet her visitors. Her whole body wiggled with excitement, and she bounced from Harry to Isobel to accept their cuddles, then zoomed off around the room, before skipping over for more attention from them both.

"She's got a lot of energy," said the dog handler. "Are you sure you can manage her? We want her to go to the right home. It's so unsettling for a dog to be returned to us after transitioning to a new family."

Harry assured her that Bea was most definitely the dog for him. He needed a dog that could keep up when he was out riding, and a dog that would be happy trapsing around the fields with him mending fences, feeding horses, and accompanying him as he did all the general chores that came with running a horse business. A couch potato was not what he was after in the slightest. And he knew that once Bea was exercised correctly and mentally stimulated, she'd learn how to relax in the evenings at home.

Everything about Bea made Harry want her. Her enthusiasm for life, her willingness to start afresh with a new family after things didn't work out the first time round, and her trusting nature that allowed herself to relax right into Harry's arms for a cuddle. He adored her from the moment he laid eyes on her. And he knew that the bundle of energy bouncing around him would have no qualms about living in a caravan! No doubt she would find it all a great adventure and the start of her new life with him.

The rescue centre sold everything he could possibly need for Bea, and after an enjoyable ten minutes with Isobel choosing a red collar and lead, red checked bed, two stainless steel food bowls, and a huge bag of dog food, he paid the bill. He walked out of the centre with Bea trotting along at his heels, excited for the adventures ahead of them.

It was getting late by the time they headed for home. Isobel chose to sit on the back seat with Bea, and he could see in his rear-view mirror Isobel softly stroking her ears as Bea snoozed with her head in Isobel's lap. It was a scene he wished he would be able to witness time and again, but it was not to be. At least he could store this memory away for ever and remember the day he brought Bea home with Isobel. Both the memory, and the feeling of utter contentedness in that moment, could never be taken away from him.

Harry offered to take Isobel straight to the yard so she could do her evening chores for Christopher. Then he would take her home. They arrived at Hill Valley to find Cassie and Poppy huddled together in deep conversation on the yard.

"You're home! Finally!" Poppy called out.

"I've got a plan I need to discuss with you both," said Cassie, excitement filling the air.

And then Bea clambered out of the car, keen not to be left out of meeting new people and investigating her new home. Bea's arrival meant that Harry had to be patient when it came to finding out what Cassie might be planning, as both women bent down to fuss his new dog. It was a good half an hour later, and after lots of laughter as they watched Mallie, Jewel and Bea romping around in hyperactive playfulness, before the distraction of Bea ebbed away and they finally got down to business.

It transpired that Cassie's carriage driving friend had agreed for Cassie to borrow her pony and trap to be the wedding vehicle to take Charlie and Eleanor from the church to Hill Valley for the reception. Cassie and Poppy thought it would be the most wonderful surprise for the happy couple, but they needed Isobel's seal of approval, and Harry's agreement that if Cassie was busy with the driving pony, he would have to be in charge of Rupert!

"What a day!" said Isobel, as the moon started to peak through the darkening sky when Harry finally drove her home.

"It's certainly been full of surprises!" replied Harry.

"Thank you so much for including me with Bea, I really have enjoyed every minute of it," she said sincerely, "and thank you for driving me home."

He watched her walk to her door, give him a little wave, then step inside. He turned to Bea

"Just the two of us now." Her soulful brown eyes stared back at him. "I know," he said, reaching out to stroke Bea's head. "I miss her already too."

Isobel

It was the four o'clock in the morning of the day before the wedding. Isobel hadn't slept a wink. The long hours of twilight had brought with them wave after wave of anxiety, and she'd tossed and turned in bed. She'd got up, made a cup of tea, then returned to bed for more panic-stricken over-thinking. Her time was all but up, and she was no further along with her long-term plan than she was when she first set foot on English soil. She had no job lined up, no home to move into, and without a job to base her next step around, she had no idea where Christopher would end up. *What a horrible, horrible mess,* she thought, as the tears poured out of her, dampening her pillow.

Her phone rang out loudly in the quiet of the night, causing her to jump up and still the offensive noise before it disturbed the silence anymore. She looked at the caller's name flashing on the screen and felt a wave of relief wash over her. She clicked to answer the call.

"Mum, I'm so pleased it's you."

"Is everything ok, darling? I haven't been able to sleep, and I've just had a sudden urge to call you. I hope I haven't disturbed you?" explained her mother.

"Nothing is alright at all, Mum," she replied through heavy sobs.

Her mother listened patiently as she blubbered her way through her failings of behaving in any way like a responsible adult and her utter inability to focus on which way her life should go. It was only after she'd vented all her frustration on what she hadn't been doing, that her mother asked what she had been doing. She told her all about the wedding preparations, and how beautiful Eleanor was going to look tomorrow in her dress. She told her all about Christopher, the amazing rides she'd been on, and that she had even been riding with her dad. Her mother's gentle encouragement allowed her to laugh about Rupert as she recalled his many bouts of mischief, and the kindness Tilda had shown her and the little bits of work she'd done for her friends. And the tears arrived in full force when she finally confessed her feelings out loud about Harry. When she'd finally cried all the tears she had in her, her mother asked if she was open to hearing some advice about the potential next step she could take.

"Yes, please, Mum. I'll take any advice you can give."

She heard her mum take a deep breath at the other end of the phone and then came her diagnosis of the situation after being given all the facts. She listened quietly as her mother explained that it sounded to her that the life she was living right now was a happy one. Her relationship with her father was the best it had ever been, and Eleanor sounded wonderful. Village life seemed to suit her well, and how lovely it must feel to have been welcomed so readily into such a tight nit community. Christopher was close by, and the riding opportunities were everything Isobel ever wanted. Her mum then repeated back the highlights of what she'd told her about both Tilda and Harry.

Isobel nodded along quietly as her mother talked, wondering when the vital piece of advice she'd promised would surface. And then her mother said something that surprised her.

"Darling, it sounds like you are already living the life you dreamed of. The life you wanted enough to quit your job in New York and come home. You are so busy searching that you haven't taken the time to realise you have everything right under your nose. You have a business opportunity that's there for the taking with the bookkeeping you have already been doing, not to mention the fact that you already have an income from your holiday cottage up here...and as for Harry! Why on earth wouldn't you want to stay in a place where you are so obviously happy and so clearly on the cusp of a wonderful relationship with a man you care about? You really are making this far more complicated than it needs to be, Isobel!"

Isobel was stunned into silence by her mother's revelation. Her mind slowly drew the dot to dots, and she was surprised at how obvious it was now that it had been pointed out to her. But before she allowed herself to feel an ounce of positivity, she explained to her mum that a potential business idea didn't give her much to live off in the meantime, and neither did she actually have anywhere to live. She was all set to spiral down into her pit of negativity again, when her mother's tone turned from the maternal, loving gentleness to a firm, no nonsense bite, when she explained to her that parents don't stop being parents just because their child turns eighteen. She had no doubt in her mind that her father would support her in every way possible whilst she got herself sorted. He would most likely love the idea of her settling so close to him, and if that meant staying at his house for a month or two longer, he would jump at the chance. And then she assured her that if her time was up at Brambleberry Cottage, then her mother would more than happily pay her rent elsewhere whilst she gets her business set up. Family supported each other, and if Isobel was happy in Cornwall, then that is where she should stay. Everything else would work itself out over time.

Isobel felt an overwhelming urge to wrap her arms around her mother, just like she did as a little girl when her mum fixed her problems for her. More tears welled up and spilled out of her eyes as she thanked her mum for supporting her, explaining that for the first time in months the cloud of anxiety that engulfed her felt like it was beginning to lift. She finally had a plan.

"Well," said her Mum, "now that we've got your future sorted, hadn't you better be getting ready for the wedding?"

"Oh my gosh," babbled Isobel. "Dad's getting married tomorrow, I've got so much to do..."

"Calm down, Issy," came the soothing voice from the other end of the phone. "You have plenty of time, now go and have fun. You can tell me all about it tomorrow evening."

"Love you, Mum," said Isobel softly, then she hung up the phone and sprang out of bed.

An hour later, Isobel, Eleanor, Tilda and Poppy were relaxing with a glass of bubbly, gossiping away whilst having their manicures and pedicures in preparation for the big day. Well, Isobel was trying to relax and doing her best not to be selfish. Today was Eleanor's day, and as much as she wanted to get it over and done with and ask if she could stay, now wasn't the time, and she would just have to be patient.

They all agreed on a soft pearl pink for their nails, and as the pedicurist set to work on her toes, Isobel closed her eyes and set her mind to enjoying the moment, whilst the others chatted amongst themselves.

She heard Tilda mention her name. Lifting her sleepy lids, she turned to her friend, as she chatted away about how happy her friends had been with the service Isobel had provided. She had more potential customers waiting but with the wedding being tomorrow, and Isobel planning to leave, she wasn't sure if she should encourage them or not.

All eyes were now on Isobel. Tilda seemed to have the uncanny ability to drop Isobel right in hot water when she least expected it! Isobel cleared her throat, pausing for time to think of how best to answer her.

"I could help out a few more of your friends," she replied as casually as she could.

"So, you won't be leaving right away?" gushed Tilda. "That's excellent news."

Eleanor and Poppy were still both staring at her and she could feel them silently willing her to be more specific. In for a penny, in for a pound...

"Actually, I was thinking of staying permanently...."

Before she'd even had chance to finish her sentence, Eleanor was out of her chair and swooping her up into her arms.

"That is the most wonderful news. Will you stay with us? Charlie said I wasn't to be pushy, that you had to make your own decisions, but will you? At least for the time being. Charlie and I so love having you with us! Oh, this is the best news ever. I can't wait for you to tell him; he's going to be so pleased." Eleanor seemed to suddenly realise that she was running away with herself and hastily retreated to her chair, and a rather stony-faced pedicurist who was now going to have to start again on seeing her smudged nails.

"I would love to stay with you and Dad, thank you."

Isobel watched Eleanor do a little happy dance in her seat, much to the disgust of the pedicurist! And how lucky she felt to have been welcomed so warmly into Eleanor's home and friendship group. After chasing the highs of the corporate world for so long, she was finally beginning to feel like she belonged somewhere.

Harry

Harry woke to Bea launching herself at him in excitement that another morning had arrived, and it was now time to take on the day! He ruffled her head and swung his legs out of bed. He'd learnt that it was futile to ignore her wishes. When Bea was ready to get up and go, then it was best he just got up and went with her! Her exuberance for life was infectious, and with today being Charlie and Eleanor's wedding day, and with it the end of Isobel's time in Cornwall, he needed as much positivity as he could get.

"Ok, I'm up!" he said out loud to his dog. No sooner had he pulled on his jeans, she was all but bouncing off the walls in anticipation for him to open the door. And then she was gone! Harry strolled across the yard to start his chores, he glanced over at the little marquee he, Tom and Charlie had erected ready for the reception later that day. Bea busied herself racing around the fields. Luckily, she didn't seem to take a blind bit of notice of the horses, and after the first morning when she sent the horses into bit of a tizz with her hurricane speed of an arrival, by the second day they barely batted an eye at her. Every few minutes she ran right up to him, as if she was checking in. Harry would give her a pat, and then she was off again, each time giving Harry reason to appreciate her zest for living in the moment.

He heard his name being called and turned to see Poppy waving at him from the kitchen window, beckoning him over to join them for breakfast. Wafts of deliciousness met him as soon as he opened the door, and as Bea, Mallie and Jewel tumbled over each other, he made his way into the kitchen.

A full English was waiting for him at the table, and he noted three sausages cooling on the side, alerting him that Poppy felt that not only the humans of the household deserved a treat on this special day, but also the dogs!

Harry watched how easily Tom and Poppy interacted with each other, how happy they were together even with the most basic thing as having breakfast. He felt a pang deep within him. He wanted someone to share his life with like that. He wanted Isobel to chatter away to him about the day ahead of her whilst they ate their breakfast together. He looked down at Bea sitting quietly by his feet. *At least I have you.*

"Harry, are you listening?" asked Tom.

"I wasn't, sorry!" he replied truthfully.

He turned his attention to Tom as he asked if he was happy to keep Christopher on at livery. He blithered on about how they weren't really a lively yard, but it was Charlie's daughter's horse, and it was regular money coming in...

"Why would we be keeping Christopher? Isobel said she was leaving after the wedding?"

"Didn't you hear," chimed in Poppy. "She asked Eleanor yesterday if she could stay at Brambleberry Cottage because she doesn't want to leave. It's all very exciting!"

And I'm only just hearing about it now? Harry thought, trying to keep his cool. *Poppy can spout pointless gossip like it's going out of fashion but the single piece of interesting news she chooses to keep from him since YESTERDAY!*

Loud knocking on the door averted their attention, and amongst barking dogs and the clatter of chairs being scraped across the floor, Rupert came bulldozing through the kitchen.

"Can't stop," called out Cassie. "I'm off to get the driving pony ready. Rupert's all yours, Harry!"

Poppy, laden down with bags and her dress, kissed Tom's cheek and explained that she was leaving now too. All the girls were going to Eleanor's to get ready together.

Tom was next. He and Charlie were setting up the tables and chairs in the marquee in half an hour and he had to feed Billy first.

Rupert had been there for barely two minutes before all chaos had broken loose as he'd scampered off up the stairs with all three dogs trailing behind him. Harry didn't know whether he should laugh or cry.

Three hours later, Rupert, scrubbed to within an inch of his life, wearing his perfectly shiny bridle, stood like a lamb next to Harry in the church. He had to hand it to him, the mischief maker certainly knew how to put on a show, and anyone who didn't know the real Rupert would think what a darling little thing he was...but Harry knew better.

Harry listened intently as Charlie and Eleanor, who looked as lovely as could be in her simple cream dress, exchanged their vows in front of their closest friends and family. His eyes drifted over to Isobel. He'd never seen anyone so beautiful in all his life. Her floor length, soft pink dress hugged her slim figure, and her thick, shoulder length chestnut hair framed her pretty face to perfection. *And she was staying!* She must have felt him staring because she soon turned around and caught his eye. She smiled softly, right at him, and Harry ached to hold her in his arms.

Rupert was in his element when the time came to take pictures outside of the church. Everyone wanted to have their photograph taken with him, and he was the star of the show, standing proud as punch between Eleanor and Charlie for their first family photo as man and wife. His time in the spotlight was hindered somewhat when Cassie turned up with a gleaming grey pony, so light he was almost white. His immaculate leather harness glistened in the sunshine, and he stood tall and proud at the bottom of the church steps, ready to escort the newlyweds to their reception in his smart carriage.

Eleanor squealed in delight, scooped up her dress and accepted Charlie's hand as he helped her into the open-top buggy. Harry waved, along with the rest of the wedding party, as the elegant pony trotted off into the distance.

The speeches sparked the perfect note of sincerity and humour, and Charlie held them all in suspense with his cryptic request for everyone to meet back at the yard after breakfast the next day but refused point blank to share any other snippet of information. The first dance captivated everyone's attention as Charlie and Eleanor flowed as one with the gentle melody of their chosen music. It wasn't until the sun began her descent, on that wonderful day, full of happiness, friends, and delicious food, that Harry managed to catch Isobel alone. Harry, whose eyes had never strayed far from Isobel throughout the day, spotted her duck out of the marquee, and he silently slipped away from the merriment to find her.

He saw her silhouette in the distance, leaning against the paddock fence stroking Christopher. Making is way over to her, he called her name softly to alert her of his presence under the rapidly darkening sky.

"I hear you're staying," he said, his tone hinting for her to confirm the news he'd learned that morning. He felt himself holding his breath, understanding the weight her answer held, and the acute devastation he knew would follow if she were to tell him otherwise.

"Yes," she said simply.

He held her gaze, then slowly reached out his hand and traced her bare arm with his fingers. He felt her shiver, the night-time sky having brought a chill to the air, and he pulled her into his arms, shielding her from the cold. He felt the weight of her slender body relaxing against his, and with his heart hammering in his chest, gently lifted her chin before tentatively brushing his lips against hers.

"I'm pleased you're staying," he murmured.

"So am I," she whispered, then lifting herself up on tiptoes, she placed her lips against his and kissed him back.

Harry's mind filtered through all that had happened over the last year. The heartache and rejection he'd suffered, his own reckless behaviours that landed him in hospital, the stress and anxiety of trying to find his place back home; it really had been a testing year. But as he stood with Isobel in contented silence, his arms wrapped tightly around her until the moon bloomed in the sky above, bathing them under her silvery glow, he felt a sense of peace settle within him. He'd found his place in the world, and it was right here, at home, with Isobel by his side.

Isobel

Isobel, along with Harry, Poppy, Tom and Eleanor, were loitering on the yard, chatting amongst themselves about the wonderful day they had all shared yesterday, whilst waiting for Charlie. Isobel was absolutely bursting to tell Eleanor about her and Harry becoming officially a couple last night but today was not the day. Today was Charlie's day for whatever surprise he had in store for them all. She consoled herself with the fact her mother had listened patiently at the end of the phone late last night as she described in minute detail everything that had happened between them under the stars on the evening of the wedding.

She looked up and caught Harry's eye; the secretive look he gave her brought the same warm fuzzy feeling she felt whenever she saw her father and Eleanor together. After uprooting her life, flying halfway across the world, suffering a mini mid-life crisis and living with chronic stress and anxiety for months, she'd finally found her place in the world. Casting her eyes across to the horses grazing quietly in their paddocks, the dogs romping across the fields, and her friends and family gathered all around her, she felt contentment deep within her.

"Eleanor," Charlie called out, catching everyone's attention, as he strolled over to his new wife with Mr Guiness placidly walking beside him. "Eleanor, meet Mr Guiness, our new horse!"

And there was that fuzzy feeling bubbling within her again as she watched Eleanor hug her new horse, then squeeze Charlie into a tight embrace, whispering her thanks in his ear.

Once the excitement of meeting Mr Guiness died down, Charlie moved on to explain the final phase of their wedding activities. It transpired that when he first moved to Cornwall, he'd taken himself off to Perranporth beach during a particularly low time of his life. Whilst there, he'd witnessed a group of people galloping across the wide-open stretch of beach, living their best lives. It was a moment in time that he would never forget. Watching those people, and their horses, gallop across the beach with complete abandon had pulled him out of the depths of his despair and given him hope. And so today, with his friends and family, they would all be transporting their horses to the beach! He quickly assured Eleanor and Poppy that there would be no galloping! It was not about the speed the horses would be going, but the fact that they would all be together, recreating that powerful memory in a way to suit them all.

Isobel had to hand it to her father; he certainly knew how to make an already special occasion extra wonderful for them all. The yard became a hubbub of activity as they bustled around getting their horses ready, before loading them up into the trailers.

Harry took charge of which horse went in which trailer, and with Christopher being loaded alongside Harry's chosen riding school horse, Walter, she slipped into the front seat of his Land Rover, excited to have him to herself for the hour's journey to the beach. Harry waited for Charlie and Eleanor to drive off first, leading the way. Then Tom and Poppy followed behind, and just as they turned out of the drive, and out of view, he leaned over and kissed her.

"I've been waiting all morning to do that," he said softly.

Isobel felt herself blush at the newness of it all, and the excitement that she could lean into him and brush her lips against his, whenever she wanted too.

Isobel felt her heart fill will love when another surprise for Eleanor revealed itself as they all pulled up into the carpark for the beach. Waiting in the carpark was Tilda, and standing next to her, proudly wearing his packsaddle and panniers, was Rupert. His large ears twitched forwards and backwards as he took in the unfamiliar surroundings.

"I chose Walter to ride, and Rodney for your dad deliberately," Harry explained to Isobel. "Charlie's been bringing that little rascal up to the yard for weeks now to make sure all the horses here today are well socialised with him before today's ride. He certainly knows how to put a plan into action!"

It was a perfectly clear spring day with the sun shining boldly over the sprawling Cornish beach, without a cloud in the sky. The riders climbed into their saddles and Poppy and Tilda, the non-riders of the group, took hold of the lead reins for Daphne and Rupert, and with Mallie, Jewel and Bea padding along beside them, they set off from the secluded, far end of the beach.

Isobel noticed how tentative Charlie was towards Eleanor, and how he slowly helped build her confidence with Mr Guiness, and with it, her furrowed brow relaxed, her eyes lit up, and she was riding her very own horse across the sandy shore, with the gentle waves lapping at his feet. That was the sort of love she wanted for herself, and for Harry. She stole a look at him, realising that over the past three months, he had become her best friend, and it was around him she felt her true self emerging, it was him she wanted to turn to for advice, as well as his welcoming company and their shared enjoyment of their animals.

Rupert came into his own when they stopped for a break and Tilda removed two bottles of bucks' fizz, seven plastic cups, and seven freshly-baked apple pastries from his panniers. The little donkey eye-balled the large horses, quietly towering above him, just to let them know that he was the star of the show. It was him who'd carried the all-important picnic for his people, and they'd do well to remember it!

Isobel, sitting on the sand beside Harry, sipped her fizz, then closed her eyes, tilted her head back, and felt the warmth of the sun on her face. The sound of the ocean, lapping against the shore, lulled her into complete relaxation. Without thinking, she gently rested her head against Harry's shoulder, her mind filled with happy thoughts of the days ahead. Setting up her new business, the long summer that stretched out before her to be filled with riding and picnics, and when the Cornish trees began to shed their leaves, and bitter wind and lashing rain replaced the soft warmth of the summers sun, she imagined her and Harry, cosied up together in front of a roaring log fire.

It was Harry gently shaking her that roused her from her happy place, and opening her eyes, she found all eyes to be on her, then they flicked to Harry, then back to her. Isobel realised that her intimate gesture had well and truly let the cat out of the bag. She sat up straight, averted her gaze, and dusted the sand off herself. She felt Harry's arm slip behind her waist, and on looking up, she was met with Eleanor's kind eyes, and without any words being spoken, she felt her place cement itself in their tightknit group as her father, and each one of her new friends, smiled warmly right at her.

The time had come to pack away their things, and head home. Isobel watched Harry take Tom aside and mutter amongst themselves in hushed tones. As she tightened Christopher's girth in preparation to ride, Harry announced to the group that they were all to go on ahead, he and Isobel would catch them up. Isobel became further intrigued when Tom swung his leg over Walter instead of Billy.

When everyone left for the walk home, the dogs enjoying every minute of splashing through the waves and playing chase across the sand, Harry took her in his arms and held her closely too him. Inhaling his musky aftershave, and relaxing into his embrace, she felt at home. They stood as one, under the brilliant blue sky, encircled by the salty sea breeze, in contented silence, until Harry gently pulled away.

"Shall we race?" he said, his eyes dancing, encouraging her to play along.

"Ahhhh," she said as the penny dropped. "How on earth did you get Tom to agree to let you ride Billy?"

"I'll be doing his share of mucking out the stables for a week," he laughed. "And taking all four of us out for a pub lunch next weekend!"

"Your brother drives a hard bargain!" she jested.

"It will be worth it," replied Harry, climbing into Billy's saddle.

Isobel swung her leg over Christopher, and as her excitement for what was to come filtered through her body and into her horse, she could feel his excitement match hers and build beneath her.

The horses walked side by side as they scanned the horizon for the others; they didn't want to spook the placid horses and Rupert walking calming along the beach with their racing game. They judged the distance, then asked their horses to trot along the shoreline.

"Let's go," Isobel called out to Harry, as they pushed their horses up a gear.

Isobel knew Billy was faster than Christopher, but only by a smidge, and as they galloped, side by side, she felt a sense of pride that even though her life had been in tatters, she had never neglected her horse. Her consistent training sessions in the school, and fast rides through the woods and across the moors had kept his fitness peaked, and today, they were both reaping the rewards as he thundered along the beach, his powerful strides splashing through the surf beneath them, and he was definitely giving Billy a run for his money.

Isobel trusted her horse with every ounce of her body, and closing her eyes, she allowed her other senses to take over. She felt his muscular body beneath her, carrying her safely across the sand, the tang of the sea air on her tongue, and the chilly droplets of the ocean spray tingling her bare skin. She felt alive. Opening her eyes, she looked down at Christopher running with complete abandon, living in that very moment, and she took pride that not only had she chosen a life that was perfect for her, but she had finally given her dearest friend the life he deserved. She and Christopher were in this life together, and through her darkest days, it was him who she could always rely on for unwavering support and companionship. She thought of her mother fondly as well, her constant cheerleader and closest confidante, and she was only ever a phone call away.

They slowed their horses when they spotted the rest of the gang coming into view, and she took a moment to cast her eyes over Harry, her handsome cowboy, and then her father and her friends; those people, they were her future. A future she couldn't wait to begin.

Printed in Dunstable, United Kingdom